URBAN FOXES

URBAN FOXES

•STEPHEN HARRIS•

with illustrations by
GUY TROUGHTON

Whittet Books

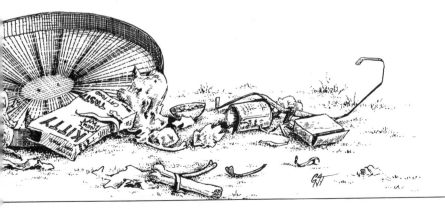

First published 1986
Reprinted 1988, 1992, 1994
Text © 1986 by Stephen Harris
Illustrations © 1986 by Guy Troughton
Whittet Books Ltd, 18 Anley Road, London W14 0BY

Design by Richard Kelly

British Library Cataloguing in Publication Data

Harris, Stephen
    Urban foxes.
    1. Foxes   2. Cities and towns —— Great Britain
    I. Title
    599.74.'442   QL737.C2
ISBN 0–905483–47–2   (M) 599·744 42 H

Typeset by Inforum, Portsmouth
Printed and bound by Biddles of Guildford

Contents

Preface

My fascination with foxes began over twenty years ago, when, as a young naturalist, I wanted to learn more about the wildlife that was within easy reach of my home on the east side of London. In those days comparatively little was known or written about foxes, and it was difficult to learn much about them. Although I found this lack of information frustrating, I was lucky to be witnessing one of the most fascinating examples ever of an animal invading our cities. Foxes started to colonize the suburbs of London just before the Second World War, and in the 1950s and early 1960s they rapidly increased in numbers. At first this suburban invasion went largely unrecorded, but in the early 1960s there was a sudden public awareness of the urban fox phenomenon, and numerous fox stories started to appear in the press. At the same time the London Natural History Society organized its survey of the distribution of foxes in the London area, a remarkable study by 'Bunny' Teagle which went a long way to fuelling the interest in these new urban residents. Since the publication of this survey in 1967 urban foxes have never been out of the news.

Today few urban residents in southern England can have failed to see a fox, either strolling the streets at night, rifling the waste bins in the local park, or sunbathing in a back garden. Of all the cities in Britain, the foxes in Bristol must be the best known, thanks to the BBC Natural History Unit. They made two series of foxy programmes; 'Foxwatch' was originally a series of eleven live programmes transmitted late at night when viewers could watch a litter of fox cubs living under the floorboards of a house in Bristol. The highlights from this programme were compiled into a half-hour programme transmitted as part of the 'Wildlife on One' series. Subsequently the longer documentary '20th Century Fox' was shown, when viewers watched foxes sunbathing on roofs during the day, foraging for earthworms by the famous Clifton Suspension Bridge, and mating in a back garden in the middle of Bristol. This film also tried to dispel some of the myths about urban foxes; for instance, in the two years it took to produce the film many fox/cat interactions were seen. On most occasions the fox and cat ignored each other; the one aggressive incident occurred when the cat went for the fox, which very rapidly disappeared! It certainly was not the sort of behaviour that most viewers expected to see.

I hope the films went some small way to improving the image of the urban fox. For me, working with the BBC to produce the films was exciting: a new series of challenges to record on film the sort of behaviour that anyone can observe in a city like Bristol on any night of the year. Twenty years after I first started regularly to watch foxes on the east side of London, I still feel the same sort of fascination for them that I did in my early teens. This book contains some of the information I have managed to gather since those early days; I hope it answers some of the questions that first perplexed me twenty years ago, and also helps generate in others some of the enthusiasm I feel for these animals.

University of Bristol, 1986   *Stephen Harris*

Acknowledgments

Over the years many people have helped me with my fox studies. At first friends in the Essex Field Club stimulated my interest and my poor parents stoically suffered my nocturnal activities and (in my opinion) wholly reasonable demands to post-mortem foxes in the kitchen. The staff at Ilford County High School were equally surprisingly tolerant of the succession of dead animals or piles of faeces examined in the biology laboratory. My activities were tolerated while I was a post-graduate student at Royal Holloway College, University of London, and subsequently at the University of Bristol; I am grateful to the staff at both universities. At various times my studies have been funded by the Ministry of Agriculture, Fisheries and Food, the Natural Environment Research Council, the Nature Conservancy Council, the Royal Society, the Royal Society for the Prevention of Cruelty to Animals and the Wellcome Trust. To all these bodies I express my thanks. A succession of people have helped with my field work, but particular thanks are due to Jim Jayne and Bill Osborne, who unfailingly have helped over many years. Finally I would like to thank Zoë Ashmore, Kathie and Mick Claydon and Pat Morris for giving me their honest opinions on my first attempts to write this book.

Introduction

In a world that is becoming increasingly covered by urban sprawl, and in which many species of carnivore are becoming rare or extinct, it is remarkable to find one animal that is not only surviving, but is living and thriving alongside man, even in the very centre of his cities. Yet thrive foxes certainly do in many urban areas. During a late-night walk in the streets of British cities it is possible to see up to twenty foxes within a couple of hours, crossing or playing in the road, sniffing at empty litter bins, and eating scattered fish-and-chip papers, Kentucky Fried Chicken boxes, or the remains of small birds killed on the roads. It seems as if the town belongs to the foxes after midnight, there are so many of them.

Yet perhaps it should not be such a surprise to see foxes in our cities; the red fox (*Vulpes vulpes*, which is the species we have) is a highly adaptable animals, and is widely distributed among a diversity of habitats. It can be found in the arctic tundra of Europe and Russia, and has been seen on sea ice 100 kilometres (62 miles) north of the nearest land. From there foxes are to be found southwards in most habitats in Europe, across Asia to Japan and south into the deserts of North Africa. It is the same species of red fox

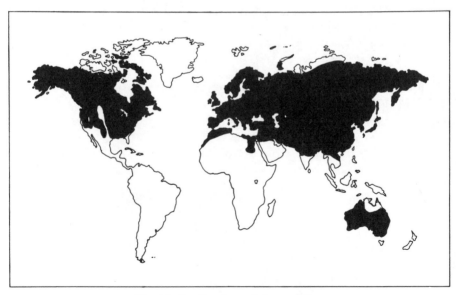

World distribution of the red fox

which is found in North America, where it is present throughout most of the mainland habitats, and here it is still spreading northwards, having recently crossed the ocean ice to Ellesmere Island, which is at latitude 76°N. Foxes were introduced to Australia in the last century for hunting, and they are now found throughout most of that continent as well.

The wide distribution of the fox, the diversity of habitats in which it can be found, and the speed with which foxes have colonized areas such as Australia, are all indications of its adaptability. There are probably two main reasons for its success: lack of specialization and size. The fox is a medium-sized carnivore, small enough to be unobtrusive, yet large enough to be mobile and able to move long distances when necessary, either to colonize new areas or to search for food in areas where resources are scattered. Perhaps most important is the lack of any specialized food requirements; foxes can live exclusively on fruit and berries, insects, carrion, or a mixture of foodstuffs, depending on what is available. The fox is a true omnivore, an opportunist feeder that can exploit potential food sources almost everywhere. To such an adaptable animal, our towns and cities were just one more habitat to invade.

At various times, these city-dwelling foxes have been called 'town foxes', 'city foxes', 'urban foxes' or 'suburban foxes'. These terms have not been used to imply any differences between the animals, and merely reflect the personal preferences of the writers. Many country dwellers (and particularly the fox-hunting fraternity) refer to 'dustbin foxes', which are supposed to be mangy half-starved animals which eke out a miserable existence in our cities: a very common misconception. Urban foxes do not survive by rifling dustbins (p.72), are not half-starved (p.121) and are no less healthy than rural foxes (p.102). It should not be imagined that the town-dwelling fox is a different animal to its rural counterpart. In fact, it may be the very same individual. Just because a fox is born in a city, there is no reason why it should not later move out into a rural area, or *vice versa*. Two male fox cubs, born in the suburbs of Bristol, moved 18 kilometres (11 miles) south to live on the windswept grasslands on the summit of the Mendip Hills – in England it is difficult to imagine a bigger change of habitat. Some foxes spend the day sleeping outside the town, and only move in at night to forage: vulpine commuters. Nor should it be imagined that there is a typical town fox, and that foxes behave in the same way in all the towns in Britain. They do not. The habitats in our cities differ in various ways, and in consequence the behaviour of the foxes living in those cities is also likely to be different. In this book most of the observations will be based on my studies in Bristol and in London.

Foxes and their allies

The *Concise Oxford Dictionary* describes the fox as a 'red-furred sharp-snouted bushy-tailed carnivorous quadruped preserved in England etc. as [a] beast of chase and proverbial for cunning', and this must be a pretty accurate summary of the popular view of a very familiar animal. Foxes are members of the dog family, the *Canidae*, and as such are related not only to domestic dogs, but also to a range of familiar and unfamiliar wild dogs. These include gray and red wolves, coyotes, dingoes, jackals, arctic and fennec foxes, and several less well known South American species of canid.

Wolf

The canids are mostly medium-sized carnivores. They evolved in the open grasslands of North America nearly fifty million years ago, and are rather generalized carnivores, with no specific requirements of food or their environment. Hence they are able to adapt to changes in their habitat; it is this lack of specialization, and their adaptable and opportunistic behaviour, that accounts for the success of the dog family.

One indication of this success is the wide distribution of the canids. Wild dogs were originally found on every continent except Antarctica and Australia; the dingo was only later introduced to Australia with the aboriginals. Canids live in an impressive variety of places; arctic foxes on ice floes and the tundra in the far north, fennec foxes inhabit the North African deserts, the bush dog will dive underwater, the North American gray fox regularly climbs trees, and the African hunting dog has been seen from the African plains to near the summit of Mount Kilimanjaro, at a height of 5,600 metres (18,400 feet).

Arctic fox

Despite this great adaptability, canids are generally rather similar in appearance. They have an upright posture, rather pointed ears and a fairly long muzzle. Most have 42 teeth; of these probably the most obvious are the four canines used to kill and tear prey, and the shearing (carnassial) teeth in the side of the mouth, which are used for cutting food. Their feet also are rather characteristic; most species have five toes on the fore feet, four on the hind. The fifth toe on the fore foot is small and on the inside of the leg; it is positioned just above the foot and is called the 'dew claw'. Although a few species are solitary, many wild dogs hunt in pairs, family groups or packs, and normally only produce one litter of pups a year. They have a long period of parental care, and it is during this period that the young learn to hunt and to develop their social skills.

Coyote

With such an adaptable group of animals, it is not surprising that the fox is not the only canid to adapt to city life. In some of the western cities of the United States there is an even larger urban resident, the coyote. Coyotes are occasionally seen foraging on the outskirts of Houston, Denver and Boise, but are particularly familiar in Los Angeles. Here urban coyotes are not a recent phenomenon; they were always present, and have survived the rapid spread of the city. In the last few years, however, coyotes have invaded many new suburbs and are now very common. The city of Los Angeles consists of extensive built-up areas divided by steep-sided, scrub-filled ravines and similar natural habitats. These provide ideal daytime refuges, from which the coyotes move into the more heavily built-up areas to forage at night. The coyotes also hybridize with the local dog population, so that although most animals are pure-bred coyotes, there are a number of hybrid coy-dogs in the population.

Coyotes are quite large animals; those in Los Angeles average 9 to 14 kilogrammes (20 to 31 pounds) and measure about 120 centimetres (47 inches) from the nose to the tip of the tail. Over a period of several years, the coyotes have been accused of a variety of crimes. They certainly do kill dogs, cats and domestic fowl, and recently there have been a number of attacks on people. Two of the most horrific incidents were those involving a five-year-old girl, who was bitten in the stomach and dragged from the family back-yard, and a three-year-old girl, who was sitting on the kerb outside her house when a coyote grabbed her by the neck and dragged her away. The coyote was chased for about 30 metres (100 feet) before it dropped its victim, but the unfortunate girl died soon afterwards from a

Golden jackal

broken neck. This is one problem urban foxes do not pose; although many people in Britain have expressed fears about foxes attacking young children whilst they are playing in the garden, there has never been such an incident.

Foxes can be found in cities in many parts of the world. In Australia they have been seen on the outskirts of Brisbane, and on the edge of Frankston, Victoria, one smallholder suffered extensive damage to his cabbage crop – the foxes were eating them! In North America both the red and gray fox can be found in some cities. Red foxes have been reported in the Bronx and Central Park on Manhattan Island, in Boston, in Philadelphia, and even breeding in the Yankee Stadium. In Canada they are becoming increasingly common in Montreal and some other cities. In Europe, foxes are found in many cities, such as Stockholm, Copenhagen, the outskirts of Paris and elsewhere, but generally in low numbers, although a recent report did say

Red foxes living in the far north of Canada and Russia have much longer, thicker winter coats.

that foxes in the German town of Essen were more numerous than in the surrounding countryside. Foxes are now common in some Irish towns, such as parts of Cork, and in Belfast they have been reported as becoming more numerous on the bomb sites and derelict areas that have proliferated as a result of the troubles over the last fourteen years. It is in Britain, however, that the urban fox has really come into its own; there is no other country in which city-dwelling foxes are so widespread or so numerous. I will explain why this is so on p.88.

Raccoons: the city slickers

In the New World the red fox is not the only wild urban carnivore, and in most North American cities the raccoon is a more familiar resident. Raccoons are quite large, about the size of a medium-sized dog, with males weighing 9 to 14 kilogrammes (20 to 31 pounds) and females 5 to 9 kilogrammes (11 to 20 pounds). Although nearly twice the weight of the average fox, raccoons live in similar situations to the red fox, and are possibly exploiting the niche that foxes occupy so successfully in British cities. In fact, in some ways, raccoons are even better adapted to suburban life. They are agile climbers, and have grasping front paws with which they can hold small objects. This manual dexterity enables raccoons to prise open windows and enter buildings, and unscrew tops or pull corks from bottles. They are able to defeat most attempts to make a dustbin 'raccoon-proof', and have even been known to lift a door latch, walk into a kitchen, open a refrigerator and help themselves to the contents.

Fox facts and fox fantasies

There is very little variation in the colour of foxes; the backs of the ears, and front of the fore and hind feet are jet black, while the general body colour is yellowish or yellow-orange, occasionally rufous. On the rump there may be a heavy sprinkling of hairs tipped with white, giving the whole rump a silver sheen. Sometimes a fox will have a lot of dark fur on the back, giving it a distinct charcoal grey tinge throughout. The belly fur can be any colour from white to a deep charcoal grey.

There are occasional colour variants; a few pure white foxes have been recorded, although these did not have pink eyes and so were not true albinos. More usual are foxes with white patches on the fur; on one I caught the whole rear half of the animal was white. Animals covered with white spots or white flecks of fur are quite common. Black foxes are very rare; there was a celebrated case of one living recently on the south-west side of London, the animal coming to the garden of a lady who would hand feed it. Black foxes are much commoner in North America, where they are called silver foxes because the silver hairs on the rump are so much more conspicuous against the black background. It is these silver foxes that were ranched extensively earlier this century to produce top-quality furs. One other colour variety seen in North America but not in Britain is the cross fox. Most foxes have a stripe of darker fur along the spine. This may be quite distinct or barely distinguishable from the rest of the fur. In cross foxes this stripe down the back is very prominent and there is another stripe across the shoulders at right angles, forming a distinct cross when seen from above.

Most people seem to imagine that foxes are large animals, and I frequently get worried telephone calls reporting that there is a fox in the garden 'as big as an Alsatian'. In fact foxes are much smaller than this: the weight of an average dog fox is 6.5 kilogrammes (about 14 pounds), that of a vixen 5.5 kilogrammes (about 12 pounds), only a little heavier than a pet cat. Male foxes have an average head and body length of 67 centimetres (26 inches), plus a tail of about 41 centimetres (16 inches: total length only 42 inches); comparable average figures for a vixen are 63 and 39 centimetres (40 inches in total).

Occasionally much heavier foxes are reported, with weights up to or even over 10 kilogrammes (about 22 pounds). Yet these foxes are not appreciably longer than the sizes given above. They are simply much stouter, and have lots of fat laid down under the skin and in the body. So the

Size of the fox compared with Alsatian dog and cat

fear people sometimes have that they or their children will be attacked by a large and ferocious fox is totally unjustified. If you try to catch a fox it may well bite you, but if you just leave it alone all it will want to do is run away. Occasionally people are worried because the fox in their garden takes no notice of them and attempts to scare it away by banging on the window or shouting at the fox are unsuccessful. Certainly foxes in towns are very familiar with people and will sometimes allow them to get quite close before they run off, but this is just familiarity on the part of the fox. Urban foxes may be inquisitive but not aggressive.

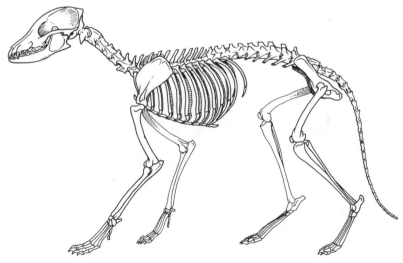

Skeleton of red fox

Fox furs

For much of the summer foxes look very scruffy indeed; their fur comes out in great handfuls, as though they had a bad attack of the moth. They also look much darker because the loss of the long outer hairs (called 'guard hairs') exposes the dark underfur; without their thick winter coats the animals appear much thinner and long legged. In extreme cases the bushy tail is reduced to a very sad, almost furless remnant. Many people who see foxes in this state report them as being either sick or starving. In fact neither is true; all that is happening is that the foxes are undergoing a perfectly normal moult.

Adult foxes have just one moult each year, and it lasts for much of the summer. A few foxes may begin in late February, particularly in mild winters, but most do not start until late April. Often breeding vixens will start before barren vixens or dog foxes, and vixens with young cubs can look very tatty. The moult begins on the feet, then spreads onto the rump and tail, and finally moves forwards onto the shoulders and face. The first hairs to be lost are the short under hairs, followed later by the guard hairs. Sometimes a mane of guard hairs can be left around the neck and along the back, giving the fox a very strange appearance. The new coat starts to grow while the old fur is being lost, and so new shorter, more brightly coloured patches of hair can be seen under the old fur. Eventually all the old fur will have fallen out, usually around mid-summer, and the fox is left with a new but shorter coat.

When a fox moults in the spring the new short fur appears first on the rump and legs, while the old fur on the back is lost later.

This new coat continues to grow throughout the summer, and will not be at its best until the autumn. By the end of October or early November the coat is long and thick, with individual guard hairs about 5 centimetres (2 inches) long. Yet in more northern climes the foxes grow much longer coats, and animals from Alaska and Siberia will have winter coats nearly twice as long as those seen in Britain. These long winter pelts have always been prized by the fur trade, and can be sold for quite high prices. In recent years there has also been a ready market for British fox pelts. These are not of a quality suitable for coats or stoles, but the fur from the back is used as trimmings for the collars and cuffs of coats made from material other than fur.

British foxes are hunted for their skins mainly from late October until February. During this period the pelts are at their prime; from late January or February onwards the fur starts to lose its condition. This is because the

Foxes are hunted for their furs from late October until February.

individual hairs become brittle and the tips start to break off, so that worn or rubbed patches appear. These marks are most conspicuous on the rump and are sometimes described as 'mating marks'; they are said to be the result of a dog fox mounting a vixen. However, they occur in the same places on both dog foxes and vixens, and are more likely to be caused by the animals squeezing through narrow underground tunnels.

It is difficult to establish the number of foxes killed each year in Britain for their skins, but estimates range up to 100,000 skins exported each year; most of these go to West Germany. The price paid for these skins has remained steady or declined slightly in recent years, and in the 1984/5 winter the average price was about £10. At one time good skins from large foxes would fetch over £20, although the average price was lower than this.

Although some of these skins come from animals killed on the roads, most of these 100,000 animals each year will have died a very unpleasant death – slowly throttled in a snare, dug out with terriers and clubbed with a spade or hammer, or chased and caught at night with a lurcher (a large dog cross-bred with a greyhound). A few of these foxes are lucky; each winter I have to rescue dozens of foxes (and badgers and cats) caught in snares set in Bristol, and sometimes even find animals caught in gin traps that have been set in the middle of the city. Gin traps have serrated steel jaws that catch animals by the leg; they cause immense suffering and their use has been illegal in England since 1959. The extent of these clandestine activities in our cities is difficult to discover, but one indication is the large number of skinned fox carcasses found each winter, often just dumped on a piece of waste land. They are frequently reported as skinned whippets, since a fox without its fur does look very much like a slender whippet. All just for a few coat trimmings. I reckon fox fur coats are far better worn by foxes than anyone else.

Interpreting the signs

The prints of a fox are like those of a small dog, the fore prints about 5 to 6 centimetres (2 to 2½ inches) long and 3 to 4 centimetres (1 to 1½ inches) wide, the rear ones a little shorter and narrower. Both prints are diamond shaped, with two small pads in front, two more small pads set slightly behind these and further out, and one larger pad at the rear. There are hairs between the pads, and these hairs sometimes leave an impression in very soft wet mud. The mark left by the claw on the front of each of the four smaller pads is usually clearly visible on the footprint. The paws are symmetrical and it is impossible to tell the left print from that of the right foot. A dog's prints are usually broader than those of a fox.

When walking or trotting a fox will place its hind feet in the tracks of its fore feet, in perfect register, and the footprints are in a virtually straight line. The length of the stride is about 30 centimetres (12 inches) when walking but up to 60 centimetres (24 inches) when the animal is trotting. However, when a fox moves really fast it adopts a galloping mode of travel, and the fore and hind feet are moved together. Depending

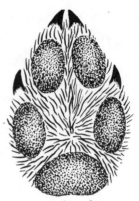

Fox fore foot

Fox hind foot

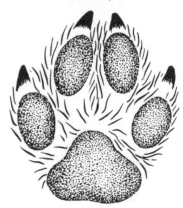

Dog footprint

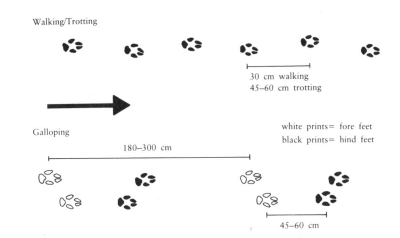

Walking/Trotting

30 cm walking
45–60 cm trotting

Galloping

180–300 cm

45–60 cm

white prints= fore feet
black prints= hind feet

on the speed of travel, the hind feet may be placed behind, on top of or in front of the fore feet, although the fore and hind prints usually lie in a group of four. The spacing between these groups of prints can be anything from 1 to 2½ metres (3 to 8 feet).

Fox path under a fence with a tuft of fur left on the barbed wire

Senses

The world as perceived by a fox is very different from the world as we see it. In fact that is probably the main difference in our senses compared to those of a fox. We *see* our world; we see it in great detail and we see it in colour. The faculties of hearing, smelling, touching and other less definable senses are less significant for most people. To a fox, vision is not so important. To begin with, foxes do not have our range of colour vision, and although they appear to be able to recognize or respond to movement, they often seem to be totally unaware of a person standing in full view, just so long as they do not move. The slightest movement, however, and the fox is away. The fox's vision is best at short range, and they can run through dense cover without problem. Foxes have one important visual adaptation to their nocturnal life, and this is an extra layer in the eye behind the light sensitive cells, called the *tapetum lucidum*. This reflects the light back through the eye, so that it

passes through the light sensitive layer twice; at low light intensities this will increase the visual sensitivity of the fox. It is this layer that makes the eyes of a fox glow green at night in the reflected light of a car's headlights.

It is difficult to say that one sense is particularly important to a fox but it could be argued that hearing is its keenest sense. Certainly, hearing is particularly important when hunting small mammals and insects that are hard to see, and a fox can hunt equally well during the day or at night. When it hears a mouse or vole moving, the fox immediately stops, pricks its ears, often raises its head a little above the vegetation, and then swivels its ears until it can accurately pinpoint the exact source of the sound. It then pounces, often a distance of 2 or 3 metres (7 or 10 feet) to land exactly on its victim: no mean feat. A fox is able to detect low frequency sounds most accurately, and probably locates the vole by the rustling noises it makes as it moves. When small mammals communicate with each other they use high-pitched noises, which are almost certainly less easy for a predator to locate, as are pure-toned calls, such as many bird calls.

Of the three main senses, smell is the one we least understand in mammals. At night, smell can be important when locating larger prey items from a distance, and is probably particularly important to a scavenging fox. Dustbins and rubbish bags are often given a perfunctory sniff, but only

really attacked if there is something inside worth having. Food remains can be detected even in well-sealed rubbish bags, and a dustbin with an interesting smell is thoroughly investigated. Foxes are not strong enough to tip over a full bin, but will knock off the lid, climb on top, and systematically rifle through all the contents. Buried food, particularly when less than fresh, can be detected some distance underground.

Foxes also have a well developed sense of touch. At various points on the body are long, stiff hairs called 'vibrissae'. Those on the face, the whiskers, are most familiar: they are found on either side of the muzzle, around the eyes, and on the underside of the chin. There are also a small number of vibrissae on the forelimbs, just above the first digit; these point downwards and backwards. When touched, these stiff vibrissae transmit the stimuli to the sensory region at their base. The longest whiskers on the muzzle are about 11 centimetres (4 inches) long, and their combined span exceeds the width of the body. These vibrissae are used when a fox is exploring new runs or holes, and they may also be of value to a fox moving through dense vegetation.

At night all these various senses play a role in helping foxes to find their way around. They can run through thick bramble patches in total darkness, following well-worn paths through the vegetation. Tactile stimuli and previous scent trails will be important, but intuition and memory must also be significant. A fox will travel all the routes in its territory until it knows every feature of the terrain. Any slight changes will always make a fox suspicious; an incautious fox is pretty soon a dead fox.

Fox social life

Most sightings of foxes will be of single animals, and for a long time it was believed that foxes were solitary creatures, only briefly coming together during the mating season. However, we now know that foxes live in family groups and have a complex social life. Basically, a fox family group will consist of an adult dog fox and a vixen; this pair may stay together for life, and will produce a litter of cubs each year. That at least is the theory, but as I explain on p.94, the mortality rate in town foxes is quite high, and the chance of two foxes both surviving to breed in two consecutive years is low.

In addition to the breeding pair of foxes, there may be one or more adult vixens forming part of the family group but not actually breeding. These barren vixens are often cubs from the previous year that have not left home, but stay to help the breeding vixen rear her cubs. This unselfish behaviour is not so extraordinary when you realize that the barren vixens are usually very closely related to the breeding vixen, either sisters or daughters. Occasionally the breeding vixen will survive for three or four years – comparative old age for a fox. After about four years her reproductive potential declines, the litter sizes are smaller, and then she may be replaced by one of her daughters as the breeding vixen. The older vixen will thereafter help her daughter rear the cubs.

The number of barren vixens is variable; many fox family groups have none, and more than two is rare. Barren vixens are most likely to be present in situations where food is relatively plentiful and the fox population is not subjected to excessive persecution. Where there is a heavy mortality from shooting or hunting there is less opportunity for these larger family groups to become established.

In addition to the family groups, there are a number of itinerant dog foxes around. These may not have a fixed home range (area in which an animal normally lives) and wander widely over large areas, or they may share some or all of the home range of a family group, but avoid any contact with the resident foxes and lead a rather harried existence. It is very difficult to calculate how many of these itinerant foxes there are, but they could form up to 30% of the adult dog fox population. Just to complicate matters, a few fox families may have more than one adult dog fox. This is rare, and I suspect that the two dog foxes are normally related. In two such cases I have been able to identify the relationship between the dog foxes, because I had caught and marked them as cubs; in one case the two animals were brothers, and in the other they were father and son.

Although each fox spends much of the time foraging by itself, the family group will maintain contact during the night. Brief meetings between adult foxes are quite common; longer periods of contact are an opportunity for play. The foxes will chase, pounce on, barge and body-slam each other while play-fighting. Sometimes one fox will present another with a feather, piece of fur, a stolen ball or dog-chew from a nearby garden. This will be dropped at the feet of the receiving fox, who may then rush off with it, pursued by the first fox, or pick it up and throw it into the air, jumping to catch it or leaping on it in a mock hunting pounce. Occasionally one fox will present another with a small bird or vole, which will either serve as a play item or be eaten. Before the foxes finally separate again they may often spend a prolonged period grooming each other.

As the autumn progresses the family cohesion starts to break down and on p.56 I explain how fox cubs disperse while the adult foxes normally remain in their territory to breed again in the following year. However, even this simple statement is not invariably true. Sometimes one of the adults will be ousted and replaced by one of their offspring, and then the deposed adult fox may move away. In other cases the whole family, adults and cubs, will move off in the autumn for no obvious reason, and then their territory will be absorbed by the neighbouring foxes or taken over by new foxes. The dynamics of fox social life and the pressures upon the family group are complex and at present we do not fully understand what goes on.

Communication

Foxes use a whole variety of methods to communicate with each other. When they meet members of their own family group, or strange foxes, they will use a wide range of facial expressions and body postures very similar to those adopted by domestic dogs. For instance, aggressive postures involve arching the back, curling the lips back in an expressive snarl and making their hair stand on end so that they appear to be much larger. When fighting, foxes will use body slams in the same way that dogs do, and a submissive fox will crouch low on the ground, again just like a pet dog.

When one fox greets the approach of another member of the family group, it will run forward with its tail wagging vigorously from side to side, crouch down with ears pressed against the side of its head, and its mouth open in a rather silly greeting grin. The fox will utter an excited squeaking or panting noise, and often jump up to nuzzle the other fox or pull at its fur. Young cubs will greet the returning vixen in this way, when they will bite or chew at the corners of her mouth, and pull violently at her fur. This may be an inducement to play, or even a stimulus for the vixen to regurgitate food when the cubs are very young.

During the autumn and winter, fights are often of a more ferocious nature, and quite a few foxes are killed as a result. When fighting the foxes will often stand on their hind legs, fore legs on each others' chests and ears pressed back against the sides of the head. Although they may utter a gutteral almost clicking noise from the back of the throat, many fights take place in total silence, with almost ghost-like foxes appearing and disappearing in the gloom as they chase and pursue each other.

Calling is an important method of communication for foxes, and one scientist classified fox calls into twenty-eight groups of sounds based on forty basic forms of sound production. These sounds can be used at close quarters and also as a method of long-distance communication. New born cubs will make a whining sound when underground, particularly when they are cold; it is a stimulus to the vixen to give them some attention. From about three weeks old this call will develop into a more rhythmic yelping noise, usually three or four small barks uttered in quick succession. This is a contact call, and it is made by a cub when it is isolated from other cubs or the vixen. Even while still confined underground the cubs will start to fight and spit at each other with open mouths. When the cubs are four weeks old they first emerge above ground; then the vixen is very wary, and if she suspects danger she uses a distinctive warning bark to alert them. When the vixen is close to the earth the sound is almost like a quiet cough, but if she is some way off she will make a very loud bark, and occasionally will even run frantically around some way from the earth, barking continuously until the intruder departs.

To most city dwellers, it is the loud contact calls made by foxes that are most familiar, and in particular the blood-chilling screams usually made by the vixen. Many people report these screams to the police because they suspect that a murder is being committed. Nearly as disconcerting is the three- or four-stanza bark, which sometimes finishes in a scream. The bark is usually said to be the call of a dog fox but, as anyone who has kept foxes will confirm, both sexes can and do on occasions make both sorts of call. These contact calls are heard most frequently during the winter months, and many a city dweller has been disturbed by these very penetrating noises, which seem to be particularly eerie on cold frosty winter nights. These noises can, however, be heard at any time of the year, although they are made less frequently in the summer and they carry less far because the denser vegetation muffles the sound.

Foxes also communicate by means of smells, and their use of urine and faeces to mark out their home range causes severe irritation to many an urban resident. Faeces are left in conspicuous places, such as on rockeries, garden paths and gates, on patios or around garden ponds. Foxes will often deposit faeces on an old food carcass, so that the remains of a hen or pet rabbit in the garden may have fox droppings left on or near it, adding insult to injury. They will similarly mark new or strange objects that interest them. Shoes or plastic toys in the garden will be chewed and scattered, and finally scent marked. As well as faeces, urine is important here, and that foxy smell frequent in areas where foxes abound is the odour that comes from fox urine. These smells seem to be particularly prevalent on dewy autumn days, when the distinctive musky or foxy odour seems to penetrate the damp atmosphere and is conspicuous even to our own poorly developed sense of smell.

To a fox, these urine marks convey a lot of information, and undoubtedly foxes can recognize individuals (and therefore strangers or intruders in their area) from the scent marks they leave. Also, the vixen's urine will contain chemicals derived from her hormones, and so this will tell other foxes about her reproductive state. When scent marking with urine, the female will squat with her tail arched in a characteristic manner, whilst the dog fox will usually cock his leg, although one captive dog fox I had invariably crouched. The quantity of urine deposited each time is usually very small, and an animal patrolling its range may leave dozens or even hundreds of scent marks in a night.

Foxes also have a number of specialized scent glands on their bodies. There is one on the upper surface of the tail, about 10 centimetres (4 inches) from the root, and this is usually surrounded by a circle of black or darker hairs. The sweat glands on the foot pads are also thought to act as scent glands. However, probably the most familiar scent glands are the pair of

Scent marking with anal glands

anal sacs; these are pea-sized structures just inside the anus. They expel their contents via short ducts, and the secretions can be used to mark an object directly or be passed out on the surface of the droppings to lend them their characteristic odour. Many people with captive foxes have these glands surgically removed, particularly with dog foxes, in an attempt to stop their pet having a permanent pong. Such mutilations are to be deplored – if you are determined to keep a fox (see p.115), then accept that it will smell.

We do not really understand what role these various glands play in the life of a fox. We know that foxes will sometimes mark each other with the secretions of their tail and anal glands, particularly during the mating season, and that they will occasionally sprinkle one another with urine. Whether doing so is a deliberate act or just the result of excitement is not totally clear. They also sometimes roll on carcasses or on flattened vegetation just like a domestic dog, presumably to add to their collection of odours. Certainly foxes have a very distinctive smell, and anyone who has stroked a fox will come away with a very strong foxy odour left on their hand. Of all the stories about foxes, the one about them being smelly creatures is certainly true. They live in a very smelly world that as yet we know little about.

Intelligence

The fox is renowned for its cunning, and stories about the intelligence of foxes abound. To be described as being as 'crafty as a fox' is almost a compliment. We know that many species of animals are guided by more than just instinct, and intelligence tests on chimpanzees have shown that they can improve in such tests at the same rate as young children. However, there are immense difficulties when trying to assess the comparative intelligence of different species of animals. Many carnivores, including the fox, have a well developed brain and sense organs, and have a long period of growing during which they learn basic survival skills – hunting and avoiding enemies. All these features are typical of animals that show higher degrees of learning ability, and this foxes certainly do have.

It is difficult, however, to ascribe the powers of reasoning and deduction to an animal, and many aspects of fox behaviour may be explained without describing the animal as cunning. For instance, one favourite story, often depicted in early church carvings, is that of the fox feigning death, only to suddenly leap up and grab an inquisitive crow that comes to inspect the 'carcass'. Such behaviour may look like a cunning fox deliberately luring a crow to its death. However, that is probably a false conclusion. I had a friend with a pet crow, and every time the dog went to sleep on the lawn, the crow would sidle over and give the dog a quick peck. It was fascinating to watch; the enraged dog would leap to his feet, and the crow would scuttle away. Yet this is the sort of behaviour a wild crow adopts, giving a prostrate animal a quick peck to see if it is a carcass ready for picking (see illustration p.113). If it is only a sleeping fox however, it is easy to see how a crow would fall prey to a quick pounce without any forethought on the part of the fox.

Many hunting stories also ascribe great powers of logic to foxes: the use of water to avoid their pursuers or running through fields of sheep to mask their scent are supposed to be typical examples. Similarly, hunted foxes are said to run along railway lines to lead the pack of hounds to their death in the path of an oncoming train. Yet in all these cases it is impossible to demonstrate that the fox was able to predict the outcome of its actions; far more likely the results were fortuitous – for the fox at least.

Radio tracking foxes

There is only one way to study the behaviour of foxes in detail, and that is by using radio tracking. This technique has only been generally available for the last ten years, and has revolutionized our knowledge about many species of mammals. Basically all you have to do is catch your animal and put a collar around its neck or a harness on its back, either of which can carry a small radio transmitter. With foxes it is easiest to use a radio collar, the weight of which is about 150 grammes (5 ounces). The transmitter puts out a series of beeps, usually about sixty per minute, and these can then be picked up by using a special radio receiver and an aerial that looks rather like a television aerial. The transmitter on each fox is tuned to a slightly different frequency, so that they can be individually recognized.

The transmitters I use have batteries that last about two years, and so it is possible to collect a great deal of information about the animal's behaviour. This is done by following a particular animal throughout each night, recording its movements and behaviour, particularly when it meets other animals. I normally track each fox on foot, and after a while the animal will become

I SWOPPED RADIO-COLLARS WITH A PASSING OTTER. THAT'LL KEEP HIM GUESSING!

UNBELIEVABLE!!

Bleep Bleep

accustomed to the strange human being shadowing its every move. In theory the fox should be radio tracked without being aware of what is going on, so that its behaviour is totally natural, but that is very difficult when following foxes in towns. They will suddenly double back and literally bump into you, or unexpectedly emerge from a gateway close to where you are standing. Although most foxes probably are aware that they are being followed, they seem to be totally unperturbed. One particular animal even gave the impression of waiting for me to catch up with him; he would periodically sit down in the middle of the road, wait until I was within 25 metres (about 80 feet), and then slowly carry on. When he was eventually run over it was like losing a friend.

Where they go
and what they do

Foxes can be active at any time during the day or night, but are particularly active at dusk and at dawn. During the day foxes tend to remain in gardens or undisturbed areas, but can be seen occasionally crossing even the busiest roads in the middle of the day. One vixen in Bristol used to cross a main road at lunchtime to go to the BBC studies to scrounge sandwiches and other tit-bits. She had a number of close scrapes with lorries and cars, and was even run over once – but fortunately only by a bicycle. You may see foxes even in busy shopping centres in broad daylight, but this is uncommon; during the day you are more likely to see them sunning themselves at the bottom of the garden, or sunbathing on the roofs of sheds or houses. When the cubs are young is a particularly good time for diurnal observations on foxes; the vixen will bring food to the cubs late in the morning and early in the evening, and these visits often provide opportunities for periods of extended play by both the cubs and the adults. If the earth is in a quiet secluded spot both the adults and the cubs may spend the day lying outside the earth rather than in it, particularly in hot sultry weather.

To generalize about urban fox behaviour is very difficult, and the following remarks are simply intended to give some idea of the normal patterns of fox activity and ranging behaviour in urban areas. For many town foxes the main period of hunting activity usually comes at or soon after dusk, and this is when many people put out food for foxes. Once the food is put out, there is a risk that it could be taken by dogs, cats, other foxes, hedgehogs or even badgers in some towns, and so foxes living in suburbs where the pickings are good usually make a round of all the known food sources as soon as possible either at dusk or soon afterwards. Often someone who feeds the foxes regularly will find that a family of foxes is sitting waiting in the garden each evening for the food to arrive. Once the food is put out the foxes may stay to eat it there, but more often they carry the food away, and cache (p.68) it somewhere nearby. Then they move on to the next food source, repeating the process until all the available food is safely stashed away. Only then will the foxes start to feed, often digging up some of the caches made only a few hours earlier.

Foxes living in areas where much of their food is put out by householders seem to have an easy life; once they have been round all their

feeding stations they may have accumulated more than enough food, and so will have little need to forage for the rest of the night. Sometimes they will travel round their range in a somewhat casual manner, checking potential food sources, or perhaps visiting a nearby playing field to forage for a few earthworms or noctuid moth caterpillars. But on many nights they will do surprisingly little; one vixen I radio tracked would do the round of her feeding sites, then often spent the rest of the night asleep on a flat gravestone in a nearby cemetery. Other animals may spend much of the night moving apparently aimlessly between three or four adjacent gardens, or lying up under a garden shed. A fox I radio tracked one winter never left a small area comprised of the gardens of thirty adjacent houses. These few gardens supported a whole family of foxes for most of the winter. Such very small home ranges are typical of foxes living in privately owned residential suburbs built in the inter-war years – the typical 1930s semi-detached type of house and garden. The home ranges of such foxes average 25 to 40 hectares in size (there are a 100 hectares in a square kilometre and 259 hectares in a square mile). These are very small home ranges, and in areas of high fox density will often overlap the ranges of adjacent fox families.

The pattern of behaviour may be totally different in other types of urban habitat. In industrial areas, city centres, and estates of council-rented houses the pickings may be less good, and the foxes are often less dependent on the easy food supplies put out by the local residents and have to travel further to forage. Here fox home ranges can be over a square kilometre (4/10 square mile) in size, but usually average about 80 or 90 hectares and tend to be more exclusive, with less overlap with the ranges of adjacent fox family groups. In city centres the foxes are often less active on the streets until after midnight. One family I studied living in a bramble patch behind a night club in central Bristol would remain playing there until the traffic died down, and then spend about four or five hours foraging before returning to their bramble cover at five or six o'clock in the morning. When they were away foraging these foxes would often travel long distances over their home range, visiting a few potential food sites. In this area large parts of the home range were rather unproductive for a foraging fox, and were not worth bothering with; they were rarely if ever visited by the foxes. The one good time each week was dustbin night, when all the city centre restaurants put out their rubbish. On that night the pickings were varied and wonderful; learning to identify the remains of Chinese meals, prawns, olive and date stones and a host of other exotic foods in their faeces was a real challenge.

Although the majority of foxes in a city are permanently resident within the urban area, there are a few that live outside and move into the fringes of

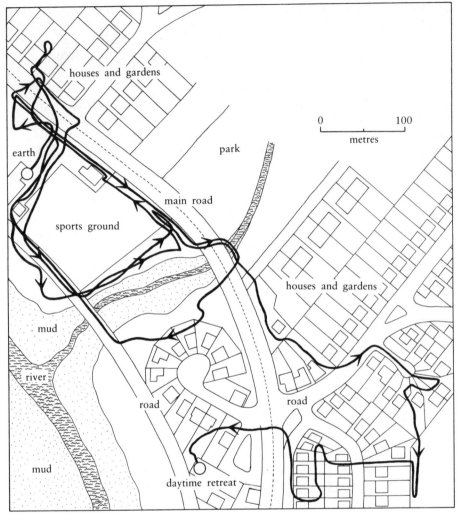

A typical night out

the town at night to forage. This seems to be a common habit in areas where there are new housing estates on the edge of the city; the gardens in these are invariably small and there is little cover in which the foxes can shelter during the day. So the foxes lie up in the surrounding countryside, and commute to the gardens to feed at night. In such situations the foxes almost have two distinct home ranges; the area in the town where they forage at night and the area in the country where they spend the day. The two are connected by a zone in which the foxes rarely spend much time but cross rapidly to get between their home and night time haunts. Usually these commuter foxes just come into the edge of the urban area, but occasionally a fox will penetrate far into a city each night, when it will use a natural corridor such as a railway line or canal bank to facilitate its speed of travel. But do not think that foxes in towns are completely dependent on railway lines to get around; this is a very common misconception. Certainly most of the foxes in Bristol never go near a railway line, and those that have a line within their range rarely seem to use it as a travel route. In Bristol we even have a few reverse-commuter foxes; they spend the nights foraging out in the country, and come home to the town to lie up for the day. If you study foxes long enough, it is guaranteed you will find an example of every conceivable sort of behaviour pattern.

The breeding season

Foxes only breed once a year, and they are able to mate when only ten months old. In fact most animals that survive that long do breed in their first year, and, as I will explain on p.94, few foxes live long enough to breed twice. The peak mating period is early in the New Year, and in the build-up to this the foxes become increasingly active both by day and by night. They are very vocal, and their blood-chilling screams and triple barks (p.31) are heard throughout the night.

The vixen only comes into heat once a year, and as she approaches her oestrus (the period when the eggs are released from the ovary), the dog fox stays in closer and closer attendance, shadowing her every move. At this time of the year it is quite common to see a vixen being closely trailed by a

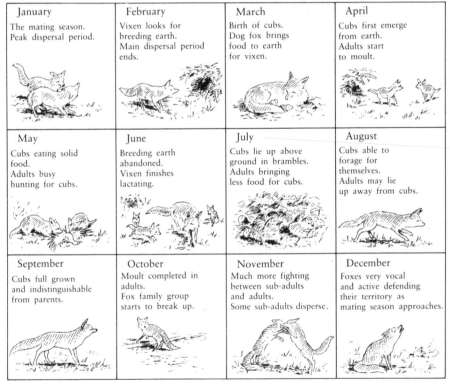

January	February	March	April
The mating season. Peak dispersal period.	Vixen looks for breeding earth. Main dispersal period ends.	Birth of cubs. Dog fox brings food to earth for vixen.	Cubs first emerge from earth. Adults start to moult.

May	June	July	August
Cubs eating solid food. Adults busy hunting for cubs.	Breeding earth abandoned. Vixen finishes lactating.	Cubs lie up above ground in brambles. Adults bringing less food for cubs.	Cubs able to forage for themselves. Adults may lie up away from cubs.

September	October	November	December
Cubs full grown and indistinguishable from parents.	Moult completed in adults. Fox family group starts to break up.	Much more fighting between sub-adults and adults. Some sub-adults disperse.	Foxes very vocal and active defending their territory as mating season approaches.

The fox year

dog fox; as the big moment approaches he is rarely more than a couple of metres away from the vixen, and he starts to carry his tail higher and higher, an indication of his rising excitement.

The female is receptive for about three days, and although foxes will sometimes copulate at other times, most sexual activity is confined to this short period. Foxes are usually monogamous (i.e. they only have one mate) and the animals will pair several times, often with the male approaching the

Fights are common during the mating season.

vixen, and pawing or nuzzling her until she allows him to mount. Some early attempts at copulation may be rejected by the vixen, who will turn and snap or snarl at the dog fox. Successful mountings may last only a few

Foxes 'tie' or 'lock' while mating.

seconds, in which case the dog fox makes several quick thrusts and usually ejaculates before dismounting. If he does not dismount he will 'tie' or 'lock' with the vixen, a feature unique to the dog family. Here the male fox raises one hind leg across the vixen's back, places it on the same side as the other hind leg, and turns so that the two animals end up facing back to back, with their tails curled out sideways or lying over each other's rumps. Once tied the dog fox is unable to withdraw from the female since she has contracted onto his penis. The pair may remain tied together for up to an hour, and can be very vulnerable. On one occasion a lady in Bristol saw a pair of foxes tied back to back in her garden; she decided that such behaviour was most unseemly, and so took a garden broom to shoo the foxes out of her garden. The poor animals could not separate, and under such a very determined onslaught the vixen leapt over the garden fence, dragging the poor dog fox along with her.

Pregnancy lasts 53 days (10 days less than in the domestic dog); during this period the vixen will investigate and clean out several potential den sites before finally selecting one in which to have her cubs. In the final days before birth she becomes increasingly inactive; during the last couple of days of pregnancy the vixen is obviously swollen, the fur on her belly is lost, and her nipples and mammary glands develop, although the milk will not begin to flow freely until a day or so after birth.

The fox family group may contain one or more adult vixens, but normally only one of the vixens will produce cubs. Occasionally two litters of cubs may be born; these are usually the cubs of related vixens, often sisters, and the cubs may share a single earth or be raised as two separate litters, in which case they live close together, possibly even in adjacent gardens. I saw a case in south-east London where one litter of cubs lived under a garden shed, and the second litter, which was four weeks older, lived in the cellar of the adjacent house. Although only 25 metres (about 80 feet) apart, the two litters remained completely separate.

About 25% of the vixens fail to produce a litter of cubs each year. However, it seems that it is common (in Bristol at least) for quite a few of these barren vixens to mate and undergo a full pregnancy; then either they abort their cubs, or alternatively the cubs are killed soon after the birth. Whether the vixen kills her own cubs, or whether they are killed by another member of the fox family group, we do not know. It is difficult to explain why the foxes should go to such trouble only to abort or kill the cubs. It may simply be a safeguard mechanism to ensure that if the main breeding vixen is killed during her pregnancy, the family group will still be able to produce a litter of cubs that spring because there is a 'standby' litter available.

Home sweet home

Long ago I ceased to be amazed at the sort of places used by foxes to rear their cubs. Many fox families are raised inside buildings, either occupied or empty. One vixen in central Bristol climbed into the attic of an office block and gave birth to her cubs in the space above the false ceiling of the architects' department on the fourth floor. Another would enter an occupied house via the cat-flap, run down the hall and squeeze through a broken board in the kitchen to reach her cubs under the floor. How she discovered such an unlikely earth I do not know. There were a dog and a cat in this house, and the dog would wait by the cat flap for hours in the hope of catching one of the foxes; it was never successful, but the chase down the hall was apparently bedlam. The occupants of the house felt obliged to tolerate the foxes until the cubs were old enough to leave; only then did they repair the floorboard to ensure that the vixen did not return next year.

It is quite common for foxes to live and breed under the floorboards of occupied houses; they usually get in through a broken or missing air brick in the outside wall. In the space under the floorboards of a house, they have an

Vixen with cubs under floorboards of a house

ideal home. It is dry, often warmed by central heating pipes, and there is plenty of room for the cubs to play. However, the arrangement may not be so ideal for the human residents. The noise from cubs playing under their feet throughout the night is often incredible (I have even heard it said that the foxes commit that most serious of crimes – drowning out the television), and as they chase each other around clouds of dust will rise through the gaps between the floorboards and settle throughout the house. Foxes may be unpopular visitors due to smells; they can also create rather more serious problems; sometimes they will chew electric or telephone cables, and even water or gas pipes. One house I visited had a major gas leak caused by the foxes chewing about 2½ metres (8 feet) of the lead gas pipe. To add insult to injury, one of the culprits insisted on repeatedly sticking its head up through the floorboards to watch the gas fitter repairing the damage.

Not all families of fox cubs are so intrusive to their human neighbours. About 40% of the litters are raised under garden sheds. Adult foxes can squeeze through a hole less than 10 centimetres (4 inches) square, and so are easily able to crawl under most garden sheds. Here the cubs are born on the bare soil; there is no bedding. If the shed is little used, the foxes may get inside through a broken plank or window, and then the cubs will be hidden amongst the seed boxes or other debris.

When necessary, foxes will dig extensive earths, particularly in sandy or well-drained soils. Earths can be found in banks, flower-beds, rockeries or under tree roots. Foxes will even excavate earths under the concrete floors of garages and other buildings, and may undermine the foundations of

bones

fur and skin

scavenged refuse

bird remains

Food debris accumulates around an earth containing cubs.

walls. I have seen an earth dug under someone's front door-step, whilst earths dug under grave stones are common but not very welcome. Mourners are invariably perturbed to see bones scattered around such an earth, and take some convincing that these are scavenged meat bones and not the mortal remains of their late relative exhumed and gnawed by the foxes.

Vixens may even rear their cubs above ground, under piles of wood or rubbish, amongst piles of tyres and old cars in breakers' yards, or under dense vegetation such as ivy or Russian vines covering a wall. I have even found cubs reared in trees. In one instance, in a cemetery in Bristol, an evergreen oak had been extensively pruned and shaped, and all the cut twigs and leaves had accumulated in the crown of the tree to form an impenetrable mass amongst the branches. The vixen had climbed into the tree and dug an extensive burrow system amongst the compacted prunings. Here she gave birth to her cubs for several years running, only moving them out of the tree once they were big enough to start to play. Urban foxes do seem to be able to locate and use any situation, however unlikely, where their cubs will be secure.

Making the 'Foxwatch' programmes

When the BBC and I decided to make a film about urban foxes, we wanted to include pictures of life underground in a typical urban fox earth. Little was known about this aspect of fox behaviour, and so we hoped we might even learn and film something new. So the series producer, Peter Bale, the programme producer, Mike Beynon, and I decided that the ideal site for such an experiment would be under the floorboards of a disused house. It was a typical situation for an urban fox earth, and here we would have enough space to install infra-red lights and remote control cameras. We also needed to erect glass panels to keep the foxes away from the cameras and lights. We were fortunate enough to locate a suitable house in 1978, and were able to run cables to a nearby BBC studio. Here we could sit in comfort and operate the cameras, while watching the foxes on a series of television monitors.

All was ready by October; the dog fox and vixen were in residence, and all we had to do was hope that the vixen would produce cubs. Throughout that winter Mike Beynon and I spent hundreds of hours watching the foxes and recording their behaviour on video tapes. We were lucky; the vixen gave birth to four cubs in April. During that spring eleven late night live programmes were transmitted, and we were able to film many aspects of fox family life that were previously unrecorded.

Growing up

Cubs are usually born in late March. Although there is no bedding in the earth, the vixen may scratch a shallow depression in which to give birth. Prior to the birth, the dog fox is excluded from the earth. The cubs, usually four or five of them, are born blind and deaf; they weigh about 100 grammes (3½ ounces), are 10 centimetres (4 inches) long, and are covered

Cub about 3 weeks old

in short black fur. In fact they do not look anything like foxes. For the first two weeks of their lives, the vixen will not leave her cubs because they are not able to maintain their own body heat, and so are dependent on the vixen's warmth. During this period the vixen is fed by the dog fox, and possibly also by any of the non-breeding vixens that may form part of the fox family group. We are not very sure what happens underground during this early period of the cubs' life, but the pattern of events I observed while making the 'Foxwatch' programmes was probably typical. Here the vixen only made very brief forays out of the earth to urinate or defaecate, and the dog fox would ferry food to her. He spent most of the time outside the earth, but periodically would cautiously enter with food, announcing his arrival with a very subdued woofing noise. He would deposit the food near the vixen, and rapidly retreat.

Dog fox bringing food to vixen

After two weeks the cubs' ears and eyes are open; the eyes are at first blue in colour, and the cubs have very poor vision. They also slowly develop the ability to crawl, very unsteadily at first, as they slowly start to make short excursions around the earth. The vixen will get up repeatedly to retrieve her straying offspring, but from three weeks onwards it is fairly clear that she is fighting a losing battle. Often I sat and watched the 'Foxwatch' vixen calling to her cubs with a low sharp bark as they all vanished in different directions, and if they ignored her (as they invariably did), she would slowly collect them all up again. Once the cubs were away from the vixen they would utter small, high-pitched triple barks that serve to maintain contact with each other and the vixen.

The cubs first appear above ground when they are four weeks old; this is usually in late April or early May. The cubs are very cautious for the first week or so, and rarely move far from the earth. They are still a dark chocolate brown colour, but are beginning to moult and patches of reddish or orange fur are already visible around the face and fore-quarters. This transition is completed when the cubs are five to six weeks old, and they are then covered in short reddish or orange fur. Also the entire shape of the young cubs' face is starting to change; when they first emerge from the earth they still have very short ears and a short snout, but in the next four weeks the ears and snout rapidly elongate to produce the typical foxy face.

Cub at 4–5 weeks and (opposite) *at 7–8 weeks*

Young fox cubs are very boisterous and spend a lot of time playing around the earth. While chasing each other, engaging in mock fights and generally romping about, they flatten a large play area. In a garden they may trample flower-beds or vegetable patches, and generally create havoc. Each spring fox cubs get entangled in pea or bean netting and injure themselves jumping onto glass cloches. They find the polythene tunnels used by some gardeners particularly fascinating, chewing them, jumping onto them and playing hide and seek inside them. The crops the tunnels are designed to protect just do not stand a chance. Neither do pot plants left in the garden; these will be carried away and used as mock prey items, being repeatedly thrown into the air and pounced upon until nothing remains.

The cubs grow rapidly; they weigh about 600 to 700 grammes (1$\frac{1}{2}$ to 1$\frac{3}{4}$ pounds) and look like small puppies when they first emerge from the earth in early May, yet by the end of September the cubs will have reached adult weight, approximately an eight-fold increase. Also by the end of September their short cub coats and sparsely furred tails have been replaced by the longer, thicker fur and beautiful bushy tail of an adult fox. In a remarkably short time the cubs are indistinguishable from their parents.

Cub grub

For the first four weeks of life the cubs are totally dependent on the vixen's milk. When she is lactating all the belly fur is lost, and the eight nipples are clearly visible in four pairs along her belly. If the litter is small, often only the rear one or two pairs of teats develop and produce milk. While they are young the cubs are suckled with their mother lying down, but as the cubs get older the vixen stands up to allow them to suck.

From four weeks onwards, the cubs start to take solid food. They may first of all eat food regurgitated by the vixen or straight away start chewing old meat bones, bread and small birds, making exaggerated chewing motions with the teeth in the side of their mouths. Young cubs often have trouble starting on an entire carcass, but the tug-of-war fights between cubs over food items may help by tearing the carcasses apart. By the time the cubs are six weeks of age, the vixen will produce less and less milk, and is increasingly reluctant to let her boisterous offspring suck, although occasionally the cubs may still try to obtain some milk when they are twelve or even fourteen weeks old.

During the months of May and June the cubs still live in or near an earth, and the adults bring them a steady supply of food. All the adult members of the family group may help to feed the cubs, and around the earth the remains of small birds, pets, pigeons, chickens, squirrels, hedgehogs, rats and vast numbers of meat bones accumulate. Also food wrappers, chip papers and Kentucky Fried Chicken boxes are brought back for the cubs to chew and play with; one earth in Bristol contained over forty chicken boxes, and the cubs will often eat the grease-soaked paper and even the cardboard box. This rubbish smells and can attract large numbers of flies, often to the consternation of the local residents.

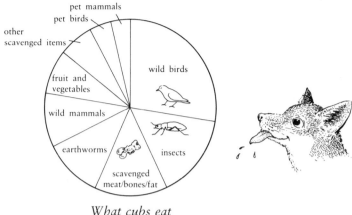

What cubs eat

The adult foxes also bring a wide assortment of play items back to the earth; these are usually things the cubs might like to chew. Golf, tennis and cricket balls are common, as are stolen dog chews, shoes, gardening gloves and items stolen from washing lines. If there is a litter of cubs nearby, be careful what you leave out in your garden.

Even in early May the cubs will start to collect some food for themselves. On wet nights cubs only eight weeks old will forage for earthworms with their parents (p.62), and whilst playing around the earth the cubs will catch and eat beetles, other insects and even small fledgling birds.

In late May or early June the weather usually becomes more settled, and hotter. Most litters of cubs are then moved away from underground earths and from under sheds to cooler localities; they may lie up above ground in dense bramble patches, in heaps of rubbish, or in old outbuildings or coal sheds. At these sites more food debris accumulates, but as the summer progresses the amount of food brought back for the cubs gets less and less. The cubs become more independent, foraging either by themselves or with other cubs or the adults. Although the cubs are able to feed themselves during the summer, they are less successful at foraging than the adults, and so they concentrate on more easily obtained food supplies. Hence they eat more earthworms, insects, fruit and scavenged food. It is not until the autumn that the young foxes will have fully developed their hunting skills and are ready to leave the family group.

What happens to the cubs?

Foxes are very prolific breeders. In Bristol, for example, the 211 fox families produce up to 1,000 cubs each year, more than enough to replace the entire adult fox population. So what happens to all these cubs, and could it be that the number of foxes in our cities is still increasing? Although many people argue that foxes are becoming more numerous, it is probable that most urban fox populations have been comparatively stable in recent years. So what about all those cubs?

Most cubs die before they are old enough to start breeding at ten months of age. The mortality rate is high from the start; during the first four weeks of life, even while the cubs remain underground, approximately 15% of them die. Sometimes entire litters are killed by dogs, badgers, cold, flooding or the death of the vixen, whilst some cubs are killed in accidents or become separated from the rest of the litter. By the time they appear above ground the 1,000 that were born will have dwindled to only 850.

Throughout the summer cubs continue to die from a variety of accidents. Many are run over, but some die from infections or are killed by dogs, cats, people, cold and a variety of misadventures. For instance, some get entangled in bean netting, wrapped up in washing lines, trapped between fence palings or drowned in swimming pools. Only 620 cubs will survive to the end of September, by which time they are full grown and best described as sub-adults.

From late summer onwards, the cohesion of the family group weakens. Some of the sub-adults stay to replace dead parents (see pp. 58 and 94), but many of the young foxes will leave the family group in the winter and move off to find their own home range. It is difficult to discover exactly what causes the sub-adults to leave the comparative security of their home and move across unknown areas in search of another place to live, but there must be some sort of pressure from the other foxes in the family group. This could be direct aggression, or it may be that the younger foxes are progressively excluded from the main areas and best feeding places on the family range.

To study how foxes disperse, we can use two techniques. By late summer the cubs are virtually full grown, and are then big enough to be safely caught and fitted with a collar carrying a small radio transmitter; these animals can then be studied in great detail, and every aspect of their behaviour before, during and after dispersal can be monitored (see p.35). In addition, a useful technique is to catch young fox cubs and mark them with

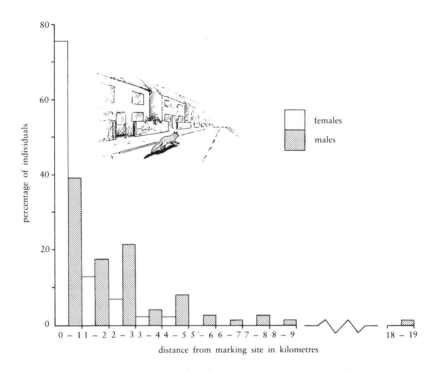

females
males

0 – 1 1 – 2 2 – 3 3 – 4 4 – 5 5 – 6 6 – 7 7 – 8 8 – 9   18 – 19

distance from marking site in kilometres

Distances moved by dispersing foxes in Bristol

a numbered tag attached to each ear. This is best done in May and June, when the litters of cubs are fairly easy to locate. The tags do not cause any distress, and the cubs are quickly returned to their earth. Many of these tagged foxes will never be seen again. In Bristol, however, I have a large network of 'informers' in the police, council cleansing departments and the public who report tagged foxes found dead or killed on the roads, and I eventually recover the corpses of nearly 50% of the cubs I tag. Although these mark-recapture studies are very labour-intensive operations, as a result of several years' work I have been able to compile a clear picture of fox dispersal behaviour. The following observations are based on the results of my radio tracking and cub-marking studies in Bristol; I have yet to see how typical these observations are for other British cities.

From studies in many parts of the world, it is clear that the distance foxes disperse is related to population density; the lower the fox population density the further the foxes will move. So in very low fox densities in parts of Europe exceptional fox movements will exceed 100 kilometres (62 miles), and distances of over 250 kilometres (155 miles) have been recorded in parts of North America. In Britain movements of over 40 kilometres (25 miles) are rare, even in hill areas where fox numbers are low. In urban areas fox densities are the highest so far recorded, and we would expect that dispersal distances would be very small. This is exactly what the Bristol study has found. Among the sub-adults, males move further than females: the average recovery distance for males is 1.8 kilometres (just over a mile) and for females 0.6 kilometres (about a third of a mile). Few foxes disperse more than 5 kilometres (3 miles). Not only do urban foxes move shorter distances, but fewer of them actually leave home. In rural areas virtually all the juvenile males and most females disperse; in Bristol, however, approximately 80% of sub-adult males and 50% of sub-adult females eventually move off. The rest stay permanently on the home range where they were born.

Even the cubs that do move depart quite late in the season. In the countryside dispersal starts in the early autumn, and is largely completed by the turn of the year. Disturbance, especially by fox hunting, may be particularly important in splitting up fox families and accelerating dispersal of the juveniles. This is in fact one of the aims of a process called 'cub-hunting', which is the prelude to the main hunting season, and starts as soon as the crops have been harvested. In towns, however, most fox families are subjected to less severe disturbance, and the majority of young foxes do not move until after Christmas. Although the peak dispersal period is before Easter and most male foxes will have gone their own way by the time they are a year old, some dispersal will continue through the following summer and winter. A few animals do not disperse until they are over two years old.

During dispersal the foxes may do one of several things. They can literally 'get up and go' one night, travel in a straight line either for a single night or several nights before stopping, and then never move again. Alternatively, they may move to one location, settle for a while, then move again, and sometimes may do this several times before finally stopping. Occasionally the animals will move off for the winter, settle somewhere, and then return to their original home range the next spring or summer.

Probably the most usual sequence of events is for the fox to start making exploratory movements in a number of directions, returning home before dawn. Very soon the animal settles on a particular direction of travel, and it then concentrates on making longer and longer forays along this route, but always coming home. It does not necessarily do this every night, and may have several nights' rest between each movement, but as time progresses the

Dispersal starts in the late autumn

frequency of movements increases.

Eventually the fox may take to spending two or three days away from home before returning, until finally one night the fox goes and never returns. It is my impression that these movements are most frequent on cold, frosty nights, but it could also be that with advancing years I am just finding field work on long cold nights more and more demanding!

When foxes are dispersing, they generally travel in a straight line, and may not let even major obstacles interfere with their direction of travel. In Bristol the city is bisected by the tidal reaches of the River Avon; when the tide is in the river is wide and has a strong current, and at low tide it has a wide belt of deep black slimy mud on both banks. Yet I have radio tracked several dispersing foxes that would regularly cross the river irrespective of the state of the tide. Some animals swam the river twice a night during the exploratory stage of their dispersal, and would do this on several nights before finally setting off on their long jaunt. One particular winter there had been a very heavy snow fall followed by a sudden thaw, and the river was in full spate with lots of large lumps of snow and ice rushing downstream like mini icebergs. The fox that was being followed that night still tried to swim across; he was lucky to make it, and was swept 400 metres (1/4 mile) seawards before he made the far bank.

During dispersal the foxes are at 'high risk'; many animals are run over, snared, shot or killed in some other way. By the spring only 390 of the 1,000 cubs from the previous year are still alive, and most of these are the ones that have either stayed at home to replace their dead parents or have moved off and managed to locate new areas that have become vacant following the death of resident foxes. We do not really know what happens to the foxes that fail to find themselves new home ranges; there are a fairly large number of itinerant foxes in the population, but we do not understand their role in society. So the whole pattern of cub production is geared to replace losses in the adult fox population and not to generate a massive over-production of cubs.

Foxy food

Although foxes are classified as carnivores, their diet is very much omnivorous — they will eat anything. Foxes in towns have a wide range of food sources available to them, and they seem to exploit them all. Contrary to popular belief, they do not live exclusively out of dustbins or from hand-outs. One of the best ways to find out what foxes eat is to look at the stomach contents of dead foxes. I did such a study in London, which involved picking through the past meals of 571 foxes. The following is a summary of what I found; the figures are the proportion of the total volume of food present in the stomachs. Earthworms formed 12.2% of the diet of London foxes, pet mammals 2.9%, wild mammals 13.1%, pet birds 5.8%, wild birds 14.4%, insects 9.2%, fruit and vegetables 7.6%, scavenged meat, bones and fat 24.1% and other scavenged food items 10.7%. Obviously there are seasonal differences; earthworms are more common in the first half of the year, mammals in the winter months, birds in the spring and early summer, insects in the summer and fruit in the autumn. However, seasonal changes in diet are not as pronounced as in rural foxes, where there can be major variations at different times of the year. The exact composition of the diet of the fox is dependent on the type of area in which it lives. Foxes in industrial localities will eat more rats and pigeons, while those in more affluent residential areas will obtain more food from the local residents. Also, how close the foxes are living to the city centre is important;

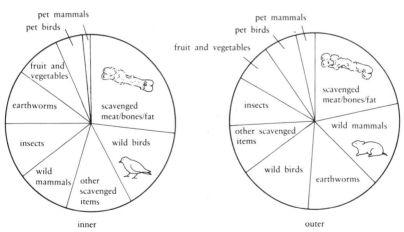

Food of foxes living in the inner and outer parts of London

in London I discovered that foxes nearer the city centre ate fewer earth-worms, domestic pets and wild animals, but more scavenged food, than foxes found closer to the suburban fringe.

Under these rather broad groupings, the composition of the food the foxes were eating was very diverse. For instance, under the heading 'insects' were included large numbers of beetles, eaten mainly in the summer, cutworms (the caterpillars of noctuid moths), which are frequently eaten in the spring and autumn, and adult craneflies (daddy-long-legs). In the autumn craneflies are numerous, and descend on wet lawns to lay their eggs at night. Here the foxes will literally hoover them up, sometimes several hundred in a night. There may not seem to be much meat on a cranefly, but in quantity they are very nutritious and well worthwhile for a fox to eat, provided that plenty are available at once. Lawns are also a good source of earthworms, which come to the surface on warm wet nights to feed or mate. The foxes will criss-cross the lawn, picking the earthworms off the surface – hundreds on a good night. Foxes may eat the most disgusting things. For instance they seem to relish rat-tailed maggots; these are the larvae of hoverflies and are only found in sewage or stagnant water.

Of the vertebrates eaten, the most important mammal is the short-tailed field vole, which is common in urban areas. Foxes hunt them in short

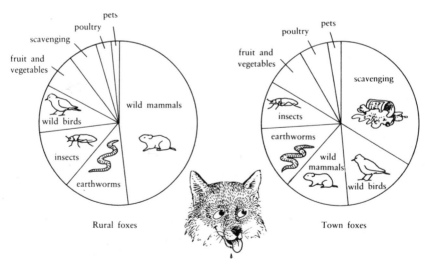

Food of rural and urban foxes

grassland on railway banks, rough fields and allotments. In towns brown rats tend to live in buildings or sewers, and so are only occasionally caught and eaten by foxes. Squirrels and hedgehogs are most likely to be eaten as road casualty carcasses; foxes might occasionally catch the odd unwary squirrel or breach the defences of a live hedgehog, but generally would not find such animals easy prey. No potential food source is wasted, and dead or dying foxes are occasionally cannibalized. A whole range of small birds – blackbirds, thrushes, starlings, sparrows and feral pigeons – are common prey items. Foxes find these birds particularly easy to catch in gardens where they have been lured to scraps left on the lawn. In the early summer moulting and fledgling birds are easy targets, especially when the young have just left the nest and are not able to fly very well.

Other potentially easy targets include many of the pets people keep in their gardens; rabbits, guinea pigs, chickens, ducks and even racing pigeons can be killed. Foxes have even been known to take goldfish and frogs from garden ponds. However, as I will explain on p.65, the number of pets taken is surprisingly low, and, contrary to all popular beliefs, very few cats.

For some of the year, fruit and vegetables form a significant part of the diet. Windfall apples, plums and pears are frequently consumed in the autumn, blackberries, gooseberries, strawberries and other soft fruits in the

late summer, and even tomatoes, cabbages, marrows, leeks, beans, peas and carrots are occasionally eaten. Foxes will even eat garden bulbs; one garden I visited in London had several rows of tulips neatly dug up and the bulbs chewed off; for some reason, daffodils seem to be rarely touched.

Meat scraps, bone fragments and fat are pilfered from dustbins and bird tables, as are bread, sultanas, cheese, bacon rind and orange peel. To a bold fox, the potential for scavenging is limitless. One animal in London would steal from a butcher's shop during the day and foxes occasionally enter houses through cat flaps to steal from the cat's bowl in the kitchen. Cakes and cooked meats left to cool near open windows are far too tempting to resist – who could blame the fox (and do not automatically blame a fox, as a cat might just as easily be the culprit).

Many of the things that turn up in a fox's stomach could hardly be classified as 'food', and a fox's approach to a new object seems to be: is it edible? All sorts of strange items are eaten: pieces of leather, string, paper (particularly greasy chip papers) and plastic are common. In fact foxes will even eat pieces of sharp, hard plastic, lengths of wire, and bits of old linoleum, any of which may perforate their intestines and result in the death of the fox.

Some of these indigestible items may serve a function. During the day foxes will often eat a large handful of coarse grass (such as cock's foot). Dogs do this as well, and we are not really sure why they do it. It has been suggested that the grasses provide a missing vitamin, but it is more likely that these coarse grasses are ingested for their scouring action: 'roughage', like eating bran for breakfast. They may also help worm the fox, and entire parasitic worms are sometimes found trapped and voided in these balls of grass. The grass may also help the animals defaecate, giving the droppings some structure when the fox has been eating soft foods, although this is a less likely explanation since the grasses are usually eaten when the stomach is empty.

Although this summary is based on an extensive study I did in London, a similar range of food types is likely to be eaten by foxes in most British cities. However, the proportions of the various items will vary. In London, for instance, scavenged food formed nearly 36% of the diet of adult foxes, and a similar result was found in a study in Oxford. Yet in Bristol the comparable figure was nearly 70%. Most of the food I have included under the heading 'scavenged' was in fact specifically put out for the foxes or gleaned from bird tables; why the residents of Bristol would seem to be so much better disposed towards feeding their foxes I just do not know.

Killing cats (and other pets)

To try to find out exactly how many pets foxes do kill, I visited every house in an area of north-west Bristol and asked them to complete a simple questionnaire. Of the 5,480 households I questioned, 5,191 co-operated. The results of the survey were very revealing. For instance, there were 1,225 pet cats in the area. Of these, only 8 (0.7%) had been killed by foxes in the previous year, and most of these cases referred to cats less than six months old. This was in an area of Bristol that contained 20 families of foxes, or 47 adult foxes plus about 96 cubs born each year. This means that at most each adult fox killed only 0.17 cats per annum, and this was in an area where the average fox home range encompassed the ranges of about 100 pet cats; each fox would encounter several cats every single night. Although foxes will kill cats, this is

obviously comparatively rare, and even where foxes are very numerous, it is much more likely that a cat will be run over by a car rather than be killed by a fox. This is not really so surprising. Most foxes are little bigger or heavier than a domestic cat, and cats must prove formidable opponents in a fight. Many of the fox/cat conflicts that I have seen resulted in the fox easily being put to flight, and only rarely would the two animals engage in any serious conflict. In fact, most fox/cat encounters are usually characterized by the two animals either ignoring each other or showing wary caution.

In addition to the cats, 262 households kept smaller pets in the garden in the sorts of situations where foxes could reach and kill them. These included rabbits, guinea pigs, chickens, ducks, gerbils, tortoises, pigeons and hamsters. Foxes will eat any of these animals, even tortoises,

although with these they are usually limited to chewing off the head and legs of their hapless victim. Overall, 21 (8.0%) of the 262 households had lost a pet within a year of the survey. Most of the people interviewed admitted that they often left their pets out at night, that most of their pets were housed in hutches that were rather insecure, and that they knew that foxes were frequent visitors to their gardens. Quite clearly, the foxes were not causing big losses amongst pets; they could be considerably higher. A few simple measures could make any pet safe from foxes. All that is necessary is to ensure that pets are securely caged each night in a pen that has a weld-mesh front (not chicken wire, since foxes can easily break this) and a secure lock that cannot be worked loose. Anyone who cannot be bothered to take these simple precautions really cannot blame the fox for taking an easy meal.

Overall, this does not seem

to me to be a very high level of fox predation on pets, and all the figures in my survey were collected from an area of very high fox density. In most towns there are fewer foxes, so the level of predation on pets is likely to be even lower.

Should you feed foxes?

Many people are concerned that the foxes in towns either look hungry or cannot find enough food, and want advice on whether to feed their local foxes, and if so what to give them. The first thing to clear up is that urban foxes are not starving, and certainly have not been driven into towns in search of food. Even if you do not feed them, there are many other possible sources of food available to the foxes.

However, if you do want to feed your foxes, please do, and I am sure you will get hours of entertainment from watching them. Foxes will eat anything; cheese, boiled potatoes, chicken carcasses, meat bones, meat and fat scraps and bread (especially if it is covered in gravy or dripping) are all welcome. The best time to put out the food is at dusk, and once a pattern of behaviour is established you may well find a fox or foxes sitting waiting for you each evening. In fact they will become very tolerant of your presence; they may allow you to approach quite close to feed them or they may even take food from your hands. Once the foxes feel secure, they may spend some of the day sunbathing in the garden within a few feet of you. Young cubs can be particularly tame, and I know of two instances of children playing with a litter of cubs whilst the vixen watched apparently unperturbed.

Each family of foxes may visit several people for hand-outs, and they often spend the first part of each night collecting up their food, and taking it away to cache or bury it. This they do by digging a shallow hole with their fore-paws, placing the food item in it, then pushing the earth back with their noses. Sometimes there are special sites for caching food, and the flower-beds of one particular garden may be full of bones and bits of meat. Often the food is not completely buried, and many a householder has been somewhat surprised to go down the garden in the morning to discover a hen's wing or a pair of feet sticking out of the herbaceous border.

Hen's eggs are often cached, and these provide a good long-term source of food, since an intact egg buried in cool soil will still be edible some time later. Foxes are not too worried about the freshness of their food; they will exhume and eat corpses that are more maggots than meat and even seem to prefer their food a bit 'high'. It is quite common to find that the stomachs of foxes killed in the summer contain thousands of blow-fly maggots.

These cached food supplies serve as a temporary larder. They may be utilized later the same night, or on a subsequent occasion when the animal has been less successful at finding food. The cache will be used by the fox

Caching a dead feral pigeon

that buried the food, or it may be found by another member of the same family group; it is not uncommon to watch one fox bury some food and another dig it up shortly afterwards. I cannot be certain, but it could be that these cached food supplies serve as a family resource, to be called upon by all members of the family group, and that this is why some sites seem to be particularly favoured for caching food. If they have been unsuccessful foraging, all members of the family group know where they are most likely to find an emergency food supply.

The animal that originally buried the food may remember where it made the cache, but other foxes will undoubtedly be able to locate the cached food by smell. They can detect food buried some depth underground, and people who have buried pets in the garden, even at depths of a metre or more, often have them exhumed fairly quickly by foxes. A frequent cause for complaint about town foxes is that lawns and bowling greens are extensively dug up, often by several foxes, after the application of fertilizers that contain bone or blood products. I can only assume that the foxes do this because they are convinced that there is a tasty corpse down there somewhere.

Are foxes sadistic killers?

Nothing about foxes engenders more hostility than their habit of slaughtering fowl in chicken runs and leaving uneaten corpses, and it is this behaviour that leads people to accuse foxes either of killing for pleasure, or of being bloodthirsty and sadistic killers. Neither accusation is true: foxes do not kill for fun, but it is difficult to persuade the irate owner of the slaughtered hens that this is the case.

When a fox is out hunting it cannot be sure that it will be successful, and on many nights it may not be able to obtain enough food. So on the good nights when it is able to find more food than it needs, it is a sound strategy to continue hunting and store the surplus. This is done by caching the excess (see previous section) for consumption on a night when food is short. This is a very good survival strategy, and in the wild rarely provides more food than the fox can consume. However, occasionally things will go wrong, and many species of carnivores (not just foxes) have been known to kill large numbers of prey. This behaviour is called 'surplus killing'; fortunately the circumstances under which it happens are rare. For instance, on very dark or thundery

CACHE AND?
CARRY?

nights, ground-nesting birds will sit very tightly on their nests, and it is then easy for a marauding fox to kill large numbers. This happens sometimes during fox raids on black-headed gull colonies; here the first few birds killed are eaten or cached, but the majority of the dead birds are left lying near their nests.

A similar situation exists when a fox breaks into a hen house. It is surrounded by easily caught prey, and its normal behaviour pattern is to kill the surplus hens and try to cache them. Being surrounded by squawking panicking hens flapping around may actually also panic the fox, which will just snap at anything that moves. The end result is the carnage that awaits the hen owner, with only one or a couple of hens actually having been taken. Contrary to popular belief, the fox is not enjoying itself or satisfying any innate bloodlust, it is just adopting a hunting strategy that is very successful in most situations, although just occasionally it produces a wasteful overkill. There is only one simple solution to the problem: make sure you securely house your hens.

Are they a pest?

Foxes can be a nuisance. To the keen gardener, faeces on the lawn, the pungent smell of fox urine or digging in the herbaceous border are major crimes, while to the light sleeper or nervous person the nocturnal screams of the foxes are intolerable. Other people will grumble because a fox passing through the garden each night starts their dog barking, whilst several security companies curse urban foxes – as they pad round factory yards at night the foxes break the infra-red security beams and trigger emergency alarms. One summer a large car dealer in Bristol was furious with a litter of cubs in some brambles adjoining his car pound; at night the cubs would chase each other up and over the bonnets and roofs of the new cars. Unfortunately fox claws are non-retractable, and several vehicles required a respray. To a few people even the sight of a fox in the garden produces an immediate response, usually furious banging on the window. However, it takes more than a few bangs on a window to scare the average town fox, which often just stares back. To the irate householder such behaviour is enough to cause an embolism. Yet foxes cause little serious nuisance in towns. I have already explained how few pets they kill (see p.65). In the same survey I asked 4,200 households how frequently they had their dustbins rifled by foxes; 80.9% replied never, 16.4% occasionally and only 2.7% claimed that they frequently suffered this nuisance. In fact this figure is an over-estimate, since many cats also rifle dustbins – but of course the foxes get the blame.

There are many reports about the daring of urban foxes, and their exploits in catching and killing unlikely prey items. These include cases of foxes taking cygnets off ponds, killing young goats in schools, devastating collections of ornamental waterfowl, and in one case even chewing one leg off a flamingo in a private aviary. Fortunately, the flamingo seemed quite happy with the remaining leg; they normally spend long periods standing on one leg anyway! Such stories are, however, comparatively rare, and predation on such large animals forms a very small part of the diet of the average fox. Instead of being criticized, perhaps these daring foxes should be praised. After all, these exploits must be viewed as major feats of achievement for a relatively small animal that only weighs 5 or 6 kilogrammes (11 to 13 pounds).

One of the most notable instances I can remember occurred in Bristol. One year I visited a house which had a litter of cubs living under the basement floor. When I lifted some of the floorboards, I was amazed to find a sea of brightly coloured feathers from numerous ornamental waterfowl. Amongst these was the fur from a large brown animal that I couldn't immediately recognize. Fortunately, I found its skull, and was able to identify the animal as a Mara or Patagonian hare, a largish South American rodent which often weighs more than the average urban fox. The local zoo was nearby, and on enquiry they admitted to losing not only Maras but wallabies as well. The zoo was 300 metres (330 yards) from the earth, and there were many obstacles that these foxes had to negotiate to get their victims out of their enclosure, out of the zoo and down a busy road to their earth. So, rest assured, if you see a fox dragging a wallaby down a road one night, you're not hallucinating.

If this sounds like a catalogue of vulpine devilry, you may be misled into thinking that most city dwellers do not like urban foxes. You would be wrong; surveys in Bristol, Oxford, London and Leicester have all shown that most people like having urban foxes around; to them the foxes clearly are not a pest.

Urban fox control

In some cities there has been a long-standing policy of fox control, usually in response to specific complaints from the local residents. In London, for instance, the Ministry of Agriculture, Fisheries and Food started shooting and trapping foxes in south-east London as long ago as the late 1940s, and this policy was pursued until 1970, when the responsibility for urban fox control was passed to the Environmental Health Departments of the London boroughs. Some other early attempts at urban fox control were, to say the least, unusual. For instance, in 1966 the foxes in Plymouth were in the news; they had killed ducks and geese in the zoo in the Central Park, and so the City Corporation invited the Fowey Foxhounds to deal with the offenders. During the day's hunting in the Central Park eight foxes were seen and two were killed. Despite this apparent success, no other councils have used packs of foxhounds to control urban foxes.

Local authorities are not legally obliged to kill foxes, but in some areas councils have responded to local pressure and initiated a control programme. Although these councils normally only undertake control in response to complaints from residents, such activities often result in considerable public debate. This is because there is a complete spectrum of public attitudes to the presence of foxes, with the majority of people liking the foxes, and it is common for one householder to complain about the local foxes and ask for their destruction, whilst all his neighbours welcome the foxes and feed them. In one such case in south-east London a householder asked for the foxes to be removed from the overgrown allotment behind his house. Before complying with his request, the council solicited the views of all the houses adjoining the allotments; only 7% agreed to the removal of foxes, whilst 93% voted against control.

Most complaints about foxes are made to local authorities either during the breeding season in late January/early February, or from late April to August, when the cubs are growing up. During January and February there are frequent daytime sightings of foxes, and people are often disturbed or even petrified by the loud screams and other calls made by the foxes. From May onwards most nuisance is caused by litters of cubs living under garden sheds or cubs playing in and flattening flower-beds or vegetable gardens. Also, there may be complaints about food debris.

In England and Wales 59 local authorities will kill urban foxes reported as being troublesome; they will trap them, snare them, shoot them, poison them with cyanide gas, or use dogs to dig them out. Not only are such activities contrary to the wishes of the majority of the local residents, they do not really achieve very much either. It costs a lot to catch and kill a fox (one council estimated £70 per fox killed in 1983), and it is a waste of money anyway, since the dead animal will soon be replaced by another fox moving in to take over its territory. Nor will killing the foxes have any significant effect on the total number of foxes in the area, as even quite heavy losses will soon be replaced.

A better and more universally acceptable solution is to deter the foxes from using the locality where they are causing a problem. For instance, the application of rags soaked in creosote or diesel oil to the entrances of an earth or placed under sheds often causes the foxes to move elsewhere. Similarly, if the foxes are using an overgrown garden, pile of rubbish or a bramble patch as a daytime hideaway, then the simple remedy is to tidy up the garden or clear away the rubbish. The foxes will soon leave. This may all sound rather like moving your problem on to someone else's property, but in fact this is not normally what happens. In Bristol I have regularly used repellants to move litters of cubs from areas in which they are causing a problem, and less than 5% of these litters have been moved to sites from which further complaints were received. In most cases the cubs are moved to situations where the local residents either welcome or are willing to tolerate them, or their presence is less obtrusive.

Moving them away

Many people find the idea of killing foxes abhorrent, but some dislike foxes living in their neighbourhood. So they ask for the animals to be trapped alive and removed; several local authorities and private pest control companies will trap foxes, and release them some distance away 'back in the countryside, where they belong'. This is usually done in the mistaken belief that the foxes will be happier surrounded by fields of buttercups rather than tarmac.

However, translocating foxes is fraught with problems, and it is very debateable whether such actions are humane, either to the particular fox concerned or to the rest of the fox population. An animal that is caught and suddenly moved some distance from its normal range, only to be dumped in an unknown area, will have to compete with the resident foxes; it will be harried by them, lead a solitary and itinerant existence, and is much more likely to die. Studies in Sweden have found exactly that: adults and cubs translocated and released had an average survival time only half that of other foxes. They also had moved much further from where they were let go than animals marked but released at their original place of capture. It is probable that the translocated animals were stressed by their experience, and certainly were not behaving normally. There's another problem about translocating foxes: they may come back! One adult vixen in North America was removed a distance of 56 kilometres (35 miles); she was back home in 12 days.

It should also be remembered that urban foxes may carry diseases not normally seen in rural raeas, and so relocating animals may result in the spread of disease. Sarcoptic mange (see p.101), for example, is common in parts of London. Foxes in the early stages of infection will show no external symptoms, and the translocation of such an animal could transfer a very virulent disease to fox populations where it was previously rare or unrecorded.

When all these points have been considered, it must be clear that translocating foxes is not a kindness to the individual fox, and could result in the spread of diseases to a previously uninfected fox population. So if you are being troubled by foxes and feel unable to use repellants to encourage them to stay away, either leave them alone or seek professional help. Your County Naturalists Trust, the local branch of the Royal Society for the Prevention of Cruelty to Animals or the Environmental Health Department of your local authority will all be able to advise you.

Will they breed with my dog?

One of the many myths about foxes is that they will breed with domestic dogs. I have seen many a pet dog that was reputed to be the offspring of a domestic bitch who had been mated by a passing dog fox when she was on heat and left out at night. One thing is certain: whoever did the mating, it was not a fox. Although dogs and foxes may sometimes show sexual interest in each other (most incidents relate to dog foxes being attracted to bitches on heat), foxes and dogs cannot successfully hybridize. Firstly, their chromosome numbers are very different; foxes have on average 38 (the actual number is slightly variable), whilst dogs have 78 chromosomes. So, although it might be feasible for a dog and a fox to mate, with such a disparity in chromosome numbers it is very unlikely that there could be a successful outcome. The egg and sperm would simply not be compatible. Also, male foxes are only fertile for a short time, usually from November to early March. Outside this period they will not be able to fertilize any females, yet several of the dogs shown to me as hybrids were reported to be the progeny of summer matings. This simply cannot happen; male foxes are absolutely incapable of fertilizing females of any species in the summer, and are not interested in trying either.

Although foxes will not breed with dogs, cross-breeding between domestic dogs and several other wild canids does occur. Many of the coyotes living in American cities are in fact the progeny of hybrid matings between feral dogs and coyotes; the resulting progeny are called coy-dogs. There is also a serious conservation problem with the wolves living in many Mediterranean countries; in both Greece and Italy the few remaining wolves live close to villages or farms, where they scavenge and sometimes hybridize with the farm or stray dogs. In Greece there are also a few surviving golden jackals, and again these are now largely hybrid animals. The result is that despite nature reserves and legal protection, the wild pure-bred wolves and jackals of Europe may still disappear and be replaced by a population of dog hybrids.

When did foxes colonize our cities?

Urban foxes are very much a twentieth-century phenomenon, and it is only since the Second World War that they have become common. The best documented account of how and when the urban fox population became established relates to London, and this will serve as an example of the type of events that probably happened in many British cities. At the end of the

HUH, URBAN FOXES!! HONESTLY, HOW COULD THEY POSSIBLY GET INTO THE CITY?

Second World War foxes were rare in London, but could be found at Hampstead Heath, Kenwood, Mill Hill, Muswell Hill, Purley, Wimbledon and Richmond Park. Occasional foxes were reported in other parts of London, but these were usually dismissed as escaped pets. With hindsight, it seems more likely that these animals were some of the early invaders of the urban area. By the late 1940s it was certain that foxes were living in the southern suburbs of London, and in the Kent suburbs foxes were already regarded as a nuisance; in 1947 the Ministry of Agriculture, Fisheries and Food shot 181 foxes in south-east London.

In the 1950s there was an increasing amount of publicity about

London's foxes and their activities, and in late 1959 the London Natural History Society started their fox survey. They found that foxes were widespread and common in the metropolis, and by 1965 had colonized as far in as Woolwich Arsenal, Blackheath, Greenwich Park, Streatham and Dulwich on the south side of the city. On the north and west sides fewer reports were received, but foxes were to be found at Osterley Park, Hounslow, Highgate, Finchley and Barking. Occasional reports were received from even closer to the city centre; one fox was trapped in South Lambeth Road, another was run over in Hyde Park and one was seen in Primrose Hill Road.

The London Natural History Society continued to monitor the spread, and in 1972 foxes were considered to be common and to breed regularly in areas from New Cross to Dulwich in the east to Wandsworth and Putney in the west. Further north foxes were seen regularly in Hammersmith, Kilburn, Highbury and Hackney. In fact foxes were now well established throughout much of London, and all in the twenty-five years following the Second World War.

Throughout the '70s foxes were reported more frequently in the innermost parts of London, and occasionally were even seen in the centre of the city. One was run over in Blackfriars underpass in the City of London

A FEW YEARS AGO YOU WOULD BE LUCKY EVEN TO SEE A FOX IN THE TOWN

itself – it was thought to have been living in nearby Temple Gardens. Another fox was killed outside Waterloo Station (I suppose it was inevitable that the newspaper headline read: 'Fox meets its Waterloo'), and another was chased round Trafalgar Square one night by a police car. All these and other records from the city centre took place in the autumn and winter months, and it is probable that they involved dispersing sub-adults (see p.56), which will suddenly move long distances and, at least temporarily, settle in unfamiliar terrain. Colonization of new areas in London still continues, although at a much slower rate, and several new records were received by the London Wildlife Trust in their recent survey.

The general picture was thus of foxes on the fringes of London starting to colonize the residential suburbs around the Second World War, rapidly increasing in numbers thereafter, and later spreading towards the city centre. A similar sequence of events was recorded for Bristol; foxes had always been seen round open spaces such as the Avon Gorge, but they suddenly started to become more common in suburban gardens at the end of the Second World War, and were common in the early 1960s. What happened in other towns is difficult to make out; foxes may have invaded from the surrounding countryside, or expanded into the suburban fringes from pockets of rural habitat enclosed by the urban spread. There may have been some variation in the timing of events, but it is probable that the pattern in London was typical of many cities.

Why did they move into the cities?

There have been many plausible explanations for the appearance of foxes in our cities. One suggestion is that there was an increase in the number of foxes during the Second World War when game-keepers, shooting and hunting were far less frequent. As a result, excess foxes supposedly took up residence in the suburbs, and, having discovered that these provided a suitable habitat, they stayed and prospered. It seems a rather tenuous argument. Another suggestion is that foxes moved into the suburbs as a

result of a lack of food due to the epidemic of myxomatosis among rabbits in the autumn of 1953; the disease spread throughout most of the country within a year and killed over 99% of the rabbits – until then a major food of the fox. Again this is unlikely to be the true explanation of events because foxes were present in many cities before the advent of myxomatosis. Also, foxes are very adaptable animals; a survey in rural areas of Britain showed that following myxomatosis foxes were able to adjust to the loss of rabbits by changing their diet to include more short-tailed field voles. There is no evidence to suggest that the loss of rabbits resulted in a reduction in the number of foxes, nor did it reduce the food available in the countryside in such a way that foxes were forced to move into the cities. Indeed, there is some evidence to suggest that foxes actually found an abundance of food at that time. In Scotland it has been shown that when the myxomatosis epidemic was at its height, there was a superabundance of sick and easily caught rabbits. As a result there was an increase in the number of fox cubs produced, and more of those survived to become adults. It is possible that something similar may have occurred in the rest of Britain, with more fox cubs produced than the countryside could accommodate. However, even if this was the case, and excess cubs were forced to move into our towns, such an influx would still be no more than one factor contributing to the phenomenon which by then was already well under way.

The appearance of the urban fox may be attributable to a much simpler cause, and that is the way the suburbs spread during the inter-war years. With the improvement in transport at the end of the last century, people were able for the first time to live away from their place of work. In the early part of the twentieth century suburban sprawl began, and with this there was a reduction in housing density. Development was halted during the First World War, but thereafter railways, trams and cars increased people's mobility, and the 'commuter' was born. At first the suburbs were developed along the course of the railways or other main routes of communication and, in the absence of any real planning control, plots of land were developed at random. As a result, pieces of rural habitat were enclosed by ribbon developments, and it was only later that these rural enclaves were built on. Foxes isolated in these tracts of land would of necessity find themselves living in closer contact with man. As these patches were later developed, the foxes had to move into the surrounding suburban areas. It was these inter-war suburban developments that also established the semi-detached type of housing estate. From 1930 onwards, financial changes led to a boom in private housing, particularly the three-bedroomed semi-detached house designed for the middle classes. On these estates medium-sized back gardens, separated from neighbours by a fence or hedge, were the norm. Low density housing was proliferating; 12 to 14 houses per acre (30 to 35 per hectare) housing about 50 people (124 per hectare) were replacing Victorian industrial towns that packed up to 200 people into an acre (500 per hectare). By 1939 this low density suburban sprawl (with plenty of room for foxes) covered an area up to a 24 kilometre (15 mile) radius from the centre of London.

It seems probable therefore that during the earlier part of this century the growth of suburbia isolated fox populations in rural enclaves. As these rural remnants were developed, the foxes were eventually engulfed by suburbs. It was perhaps fortuitous that the type of housing proliferating at that time offered a suitable habitat in which the foxes could thrive. In fact, even today it is the inter-war housing developments that hold the greatest number of foxes. Once established in the suburban fringe, it was a logical step for foxes to spread into our city centres, and to colonize less favourable urban habitats. The studies in London have demonstrated that this is exactly what happened; foxes were common in the suburbs by the mid-1940s, and from there they rapidly spread into much of the metropolis in the next twenty-five years.

Which cities have foxes?

Urban foxes are very fussy about the areas in which they live, and are only common in certain types of towns and cities. They like residential areas built in the 1930s, and particularly suburbs in which the housing is mainly owner-occupied (the rise of the bourgeois fox). Foxes are much less common in those towns where the housing is predominantly rented from the local authority, and in towns with large amounts of industry. It is the inter-war owner-occupied suburbs that seem to be the ideal urban fox habitat, and new towns and cities, even if they are comprised largely of owner-occupied housing with little industry, will have comparatively few urban foxes.

What foxes like about the 1930s semi is not the house itself but the garden. At that time land prices were cheap, and houses had a reasonable sized back gardens. The gardens had space, and people planted hedges and shrubs and bought themselves a garden shed. All these provide ideal cover for foxes during the day. If there was room for a bird table or compost heap

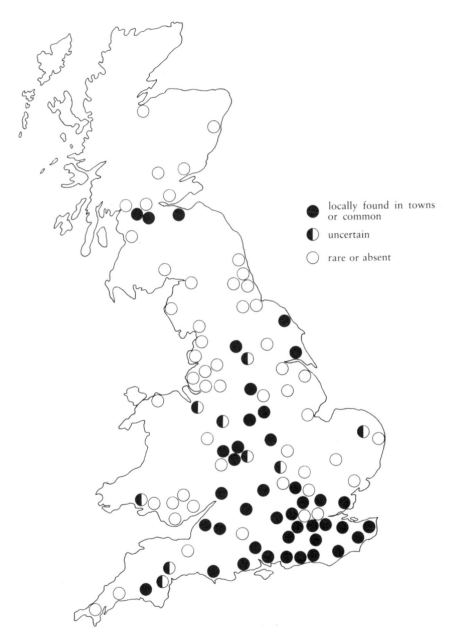

locally found in towns
or common

uncertain

rare or absent

Distribution of urban foxes in the British Isles

this was an added perk, since it was a source of food for the foxes. Older houses have very small gardens or yards, and modern houses have small gardens which are often open plan. Neither provides an ideal habitat for the foxes. The same arguments explain why foxes are rare in many European cities. It is simply because Continental housing styles less frequently offer the secluded medium-sized gardens beloved by foxes.

From the above, it must be obvious that urban foxes belong to the middle class, and will be most common in the commuter and dormitory towns of south and east England. In fact there are few urban areas in south-east England that do not have a thriving fox population. In London foxes are commonest in the south and east of the city, and less common north of the river in areas like Barking, Ilford, Newham, Haringey, and Hackney. These are all the parts of the city where the housing is relatively old or has been replaced by tower blocks, with a large percentage of the housing council-rented, and a high proportion of industrial sites.

Elsewhere, a similar pattern can be seen, with some cities having foxes and others not. In Leicester, for instance, there are only a few foxes, and these are mainly in the east of the city; the rest of the city is largely industrial or with older terraced housing and hence they are rare. Nottingham, Sheffield and Kingston-upon-Hull have a few, mostly confined to the pockets of inter-war semi-detached housing. In north-east England and South Wales the urban areas are all predominantly industrial with few areas of semi-detached housing, so urban foxes are rare. A similar pattern is seen in north-west England, where a few of the more affluent commuter areas around Liverpool are the main areas for urban foxes. North of the border foxes are to be found in Edinburgh and some of the richer suburbs of Glasgow. As a guide, urban wards that vote Conservative will have foxes, those that vote Labour will have few or none, and those that vote Liberal/SDP may or may not have them.

Curiously, there are some potentially suitable cities that have few or no urban foxes; Cambridge and some of the other East Anglian towns are good examples. The probable reason for this is simple; until recently foxes were rare in many parts of rural East Anglia, and where they were rare the urban areas were not colonized. In recent years fox numbers have increased in the surrounding countryside, and so it is possible that these towns may be colonized by foxes in due course.

How many urban foxes are there?

This is a question that is easily (and frequently) asked but incredibly difficult to answer. The problem is how to find out? Foxes certainly are common in our cities, and I am often told that there are more foxes in London than the whole of the rural area of south-east England. It is true that if you walk the streets of north-west Bristol and parts of south-east London from midnight onwards, in two or three hours you are likely to see more foxes than you would in a whole year of country walking; counting them reliably, however, is the problem. It is hard enough to count foxes in rural areas, let alone in a city, and so there are comparatively few reliable fox population estimates from anywhere in the world.

Two aspects of fox biology do make it a little easier to develop a census

technique. Firstly, foxes live in family groups, and these usually consist of one dog fox, one vixen that breeds, and sometimes one or more non-breeding vixens (see p.28). Secondly, foxes only breed once a year, and all at the same time. Each family of foxes usually produces a single litter of cubs. So if all the litters of cubs in an area can be located and counted, this will tell you exactly how many families of foxes are present.

Even this requires a lot of very hard work. I first tried to count the families of foxes living in two areas of Bristol, and this involved delivering a letter to 19,000 households requesting information and help, and searching all the allotments, empty houses and pieces of derelict land in an area of nearly 9 square kilometres (3½ square miles). The young cubs first appear above ground at the end of April, so the whole survey must be completed as soon as possible after this date, before the litters of cubs are moved away or split up and leave the family home.

Despite all the problems, it worked, and I found that the foxes were not evenly distributed across the areas I surveyed; their numbers varied from about 2 up to nearly 5 families of foxes per square kilometre. These results were very encouraging, and also showed that there is some justification for the claims about the number of foxes in our cities. Few rural areas will contain more than one family of foxes per square kilometre, and some upland hill areas may contain as few as one family of foxes per 40 square kilometres. Densities in parts of Bristol were about 200 times higher.

The next problem was to try to work out how many foxes there were in the whole of Bristol, an area of 116 square kilometres (45 square miles) with over half a million people. I tried several methods, but the most successful was to use the school children in Bristol to record fox sightings for a period of a month. Each school was sent very specific instructions on what to do, and most schools participated. This gave an even coverage of the whole city, and during the survey the school children reported 4,227 fox sightings. Then I divided the whole city into a grid and recorded the number of sightings in each square of the grid. The problem was to find out how many foxes were represented by those 4,227 sightings. For the two small areas I had surveyed myself, I knew exactly how many fox families were present, and so for these two areas I calculated the number of fox sightings reported by the children for each family of foxes I knew to be present. There were approximately 20 sightings per family of foxes, and I then used this figure to estimate the number of families of foxes in the rest of the city, where I had not been able to actually locate and count the litters of cubs.

The technique sounds crude, but is remarkably accurate. Having estimated how many fox families were present, in subsequent years I actually

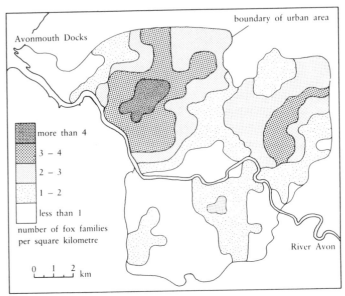

Distribution and numbers of foxes in Bristol

surveyed small areas of the city to check my estimates, and they were right. Overall the survey showed that in Bristol there were 211 families of foxes. The next stage was to find out exactly how many foxes there were in each family. This revealed that the fox population consists of 211 dog foxes, 211 breeding vixens and 74 non-breeding vixens, a total of nearly 500 adult foxes. In Bristol each litter of fox cubs averages 4.75 pups, so the 211 fox families could produce about 1,000 cubs each year, bringing the total spring fox population up to around 1,500 animals. However, not many of these cubs survive (see p.60), and each year a good proportion of the adult foxes also die (see p.94), so that by the end of the following winter the fox population is back down to 500 animals.

To see how typical these fox densities are for British cities, I then surveyed a number of other cities, using the same techniques. Bath, for instance, had 22 fox families in just under 21 square kilometres (8 square miles), an average of 1.06 fox families per square kilometre (compared with 1.82 in Bristol). In Bournemouth and Poole there were 144 fox families in an area of 83 square kilometres (32 square miles). Leicester had only 38 fox families in 89 square kilometres (34 square miles), whereas Cheltenham had 52 fox families in just over 23 square kilometres (9 square miles); this average density of 2.24 fox families per square kilometre is the highest so far recorded in any city. In none of these cities were the foxes evenly distributed; they were clumped in particular areas. Yet even in those areas where foxes were very common there were no more than 5 fox families per square kilometre, and it looks as though this is probably the maximum fox population density that a town can support.

In every city I surveyed it was clear that foxes were very unevenly distributed. In a survey of the whole of the West Midlands conurbation I found that there were 683 fox families living in an areas of 589 square kilometres (227 square miles). Yet large parts of the West Midlands had very few foxes – they were remarkably scarce over virtually all of Wolverhampton and Walsall, and most common in the south and east of the conurbation, around Dudley, West Bromwich, Stourbridge, Halesowen, the southern side of Birmingham, parts of Solihull, and in Sutton Coldfield. As I explained on p.86, these are all the areas of 1930s semi-detached owner-occupied houses with medium-sized gardens and plenty of food and cover for the foxes.

How long do urban foxes live?

Some foxes may look very old, and often people report seeing 'an old fox with a grey muzzle'. It may work as a way of ageing humans, but it's not a reliable way of telling a fox's age. A grizzled animal can equally be an old or a very young animal. There is no way of estimating the age of a fox just by watching it. However, if you can catch your fox, or have a dead fox, it is fairly easy (with practice) to find out exactly when it was born. Two techniques are frequently used. Firstly, the teeth wear out at a relatively constant rate, and so an approximate age can be estimated from how worn the teeth are, particularly the small front (incisor) ones. This method is

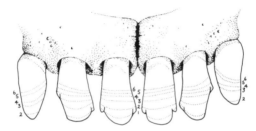

Foxes can be aged by the amount of wear on their incisor teeth – the numbers show the age of the fox in years.

useful for a live fox, but a more precise technique can be applied in the laboratory to dead animals. Each winter foxes develop a ring in the cementum of their teeth. Cementum is the layer around the root of each tooth, and these annual rings are very similar in appearance to the rings seen in the trunk of a tree. To see the rings, the tooth is soaked in a weak solution of nitric acid until all the calcium is removed. The tooth is then soft and rubbery. Very thin sections can be cut with a sharp blade and stained with a mauve dye so that the rings can be seen and counted under a low power microscope.

We do not really understand the reason why these rings are laid down, but they are probably produced in response to physiological changes associated with reproduction and are formed late in the winter. There is also some evidence to suggest that the rings are more distinct in animals that live in places with colder winters.

Wild foxes have a surprisingly short life expectancy. Although captive foxes can live up to fourteen years, few wild foxes live more than a couple of years, and in Bristol the average life expectancy is just eighteen months. From a sample of nearly 1,700 dead foxes, I found that 52% were less than a year old, 24% one to two years old, 12% two to three years old, 6% three to four years old, 3% four to five years old, and only 3% were older. The oldest fox I have ever examined was under nine. I obtained similar results from a sample of about 1,140 dead foxes from London but here the average life expectancy is a little less – only fourteen months. Clearly an awful lot of urban foxes die young and few live to a ripe old age.

This mortality rate may seem very high, but in many fox populations the turnover is even higher. Some studies in rural areas have found that in situations where there are extensive fox control programmes, nearly 80% of the animals are less than a year old, and foxes over three years old are very rare. To make up for such a high rate of mortality, the foxes have larger litters (an average of seven or more cubs compared with an average of less than five in town foxes), and all the vixens will breed, whereas each year about 25% of the vixens in urban areas do not.

This high birth rate and high death rate has a significant effect on fox social structure. I have already explained (see p.28) that foxes live in family groups, and that fox pairs will normally stay together for life. However, in an area like London, where about 60% of the foxes die each year, there is only a 16% chance that both animals will survive for a second breeding season, a 48% chance that one animal will die, and a 36% chance that both animals will die. In areas where 80% of the foxes die each year, there is only a 4% chance that both adults will survive for another year, a 32% chance that only one animal will die and a 64% chance that both will be dead by the following year.

If it is the vixen that dies, it is probable that she will be replaced by one of her sisters or daughters as the breeding vixen, in which case the dog fox may be mating with one of his own offspring. Should the vixen survive to old age (i.e. over four years old), her reproductive capability is lower, and she may well be replaced by one of her own offspring as the breeding animal. The older vixen will usually remain as one of the family group and help with raising the cubs. Should the dog fox be killed, he may be replaced by one of his own sons, but since many male cubs disperse each year (see p.58) it is more likely that he will be replaced by a new dog fox moving into the area from somewhere else.

Death

Each year up to 60% of a town fox population dies, and the greatest single cause of death is undoubtedly the motor car. In Bristol 49% of the foxes that die each year are killed by cars and a further 1% by trains; the majority of road deaths occur in the winter months. Sometimes two or three foxes are run over together; these are usually animals that were playing in the road, or sometimes foxes that were too busy fighting to notice an approaching vehicle. Not all the foxes that are killed are run over by accident; while out fox watching I have seen several instances of cars deliberately swerving to run a fox over, and have even seen a car mount a pavement to kill a fox.

It is very difficult to determine exactly what proportion of urban foxes are deliberately killed each year, since many of the people involved wish to keep their activities secret. In my sample I have expended a lot of effort trying to discover the proportion of foxes killed on purpose rather than by accident, and I think that my figures are probably an accurate estimation of the importance of these clandestine human activities. In Bristol I think that some 25% of the foxes that die each year are deliberately killed. Even in the middle of our cities many of the foxes die lingering and unpleasant deaths in

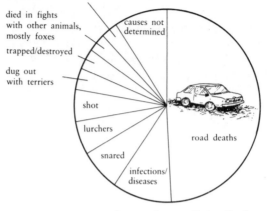

misadventure (trains, prolapses, ruptures, drowning in swimming pools, falling into oil pits, etc)

died in fights with other animals, mostly foxes

trapped/destroyed

dug out with terriers

causes not determined

shot

lurchers

snared

infections/ diseases

road deaths

Causes of mortality in Bristol's foxes

snares; this is the fate of 7% of Bristol's foxes. Others (5%) are shot; a few foxes are killed humanely with shot-guns, but most are shot at with totally inappropriate weapons. Air-gun pellets are frequently found embedded in the skin or bones, and one fox I had from London had been shot twice in one eye with a 0.22 air rifle. This had blinded the animal and caused it considerable distress; a totally senseless act since there is no chance that an air rifle would kill an adult fox. Another animal I examined from London had been shot in the chest with an arrow; about twenty centimetres of the shaft was protruding from the animal, and every time it tried to get through a small gap in a fence it got entangled. I have also heard reports of foxes shot and wounded with the plastic arrows used in children's cross-bows; these have enough power to injure but not to kill a fox. Some even more unpleasant methods are used to catch and kill foxes. Three per cent of my Bristol sample were caught in home-made (and inhumane) cage traps, 4% were dug out of their earths with terriers, and 6% were killed at night with lurchers, which are fast long-legged dogs, frequently used by poachers. A powerful lamp is used to dazzle the fox in the open, such as in the middle of a playing field, and the lurcher is then released. It is usually fast enough to catch the fox before it can reach cover on the edge of the field.

Each year a number of foxes die from various diseases; this accounts for 11% of the foxes that die in Bristol. Urban foxes will succumb to a variety of bacterial and viral infections, some of which they probably catch from domestic pets, and these are detailed on p. 101. Also young cubs and adults, particularly in the winter, will get a lung infection and die from exudative pleurisy, and in some areas mange (see p. 101) can be an important cause of death.

Particularly during the winter months, a number of foxes will be killed or seriously debilitated by fights with other foxes. This is particularly common during the breeding season, and 4% of the corpses I examine have died this way. If a fox is seriously injured in a fight, it will often creep away to a nearby earth to recover, but in the summer months injuries quickly attract flies and infection, and even quite minor wounds can result in the death of a fox. A few foxes will also be killed during fights with dogs or, in some cities, with badgers.

Other than these, a few animals die from a variety of misadventures. Occasionally animals sheltering in storm drains are drowned following a sudden heavy rainfall, or they get blocked into earths when an area is bull-dozed at the start of building operations. A few inquisitive foxes will choke to death on objects swallowed out of curiosity. I have also seen two

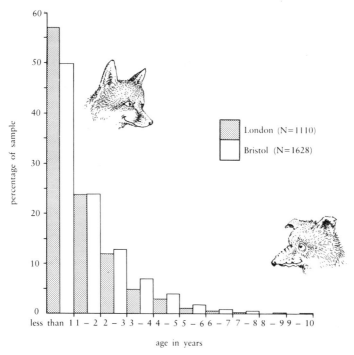

Age structure of fox population in London and Bristol

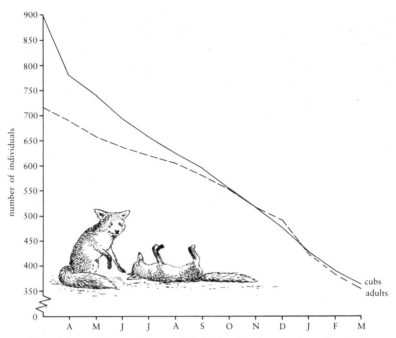

The number of foxes alive each month in Bristol – the number of cubs that survive each year balances the number of adults that die.

foxes with their heads stuck in empty food tins, but these I did manage to rescue. A few vixens die whilst giving birth to their young, and some litters of cubs die if their mother is killed, perhaps run over.

Obviously a lot of animals die as the result of accidents, and these are most likely to occur during those periods of the year when foxes are most active and therefore more at risk. With the cubs it is the females that are slightly more likely to be killed fighting over territory. Mortality rates for male foxes are highest in the winter months, particularly during the dispersal and mating season when they are most active. However, in the early summer it is the adult vixens rather than the adult dog foxes that are most likely to be killed, because they are moving further afield looking for food for their cubs. Overall, life expectancy is not much different for either sex.

Parasites and diseases

Like other wild mammals, foxes are susceptible to a variety of parasites and diseases, and 11% of the dead foxes I examine in Bristol have died from some sort of infection. This may seem high, and many country dwellers will tell you that town foxes are 'mangy, disease-ridden animals'. However, I'm not sure that is really true. In a city, sick or dying animals are quickly noticed and reported to animal welfare societies or the police, and so their corpses are more likely to be recovered. In the country diseased or sick animals will retreat underground to their earth, and probably die there without ever being seen or their bodies recovered. We have no idea of the importance of disease as a cause of mortality in rural foxes, and hence we do not know whether there is a higher incidence of disease in town foxes.

Life in towns can actually reduce the incidence of certain parasites in foxes. Tapeworms, for instance, have a two-stage life cycle. The larval stage lives in an intermediate host such as a mouse or rabbit. Since town foxes eat fewer mice and rabbits than rural foxes, they are less likely to be infected with tapeworms. Young cubs do carry a lot of parasitic roundworms (nematodes) and heavy infections can result in very pot-bellied cubs. However, by three to four months of age most cubs have developed a degree of immunity, and thereafter the incidence of roundworms is low. The commonest gut roundworm is *Toxocara canis*, the same parasite found in domestic dogs. Urban foxes will also sometimes carry bladder worms, and occasionally I get reports of foxes seen or heard to be coughing. These are

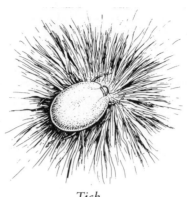

Tick

usually animals badly infected with lung worms.

Besides these internal parasites, foxes are infested with a variety of external parasites. They carry two species of tick (the dog tick and the hedgehog tick), which are most frequently found around the ears and sometimes the groin. These are round grey shiny things which fasten on by embedding their heads into the skin. They feed on the fox's blood for about fourteen days, when they become bloated and drop off. Before the ticks start to feed they are only a couple of millimetres long, but by the time they have finished they are the size of a small bean.

Several species of flea are also found on foxes, though rarely in large numbers. The dog, cat and human fleas will probably feed on the foxes, but most fleas are just passive 'riders' that will leave after a few days. Hedgehog and rabbit fleas, for instance, are sometimes present in large numbers, but this is usually because the fox has just eaten a rabbit or hedgehog, or stuck its nose into a hedgehog's nest or dug out a rabbit burrow. The fleas jump on to the fox, but then discover they are on the wrong species of animal. Both rabbit and hedgehog fleas require the blood from their own particular species of host in order to develop properly, and so they soon leave the fox. Fleas and ticks are most frequent on breeding vixens and cubs in the spring and early summer, when they are living in one particular earth. It gives the parasites a chance to build up their numbers. Dog foxes and barren vixens have fewer of these parasites, as do vixens during the winter months, and this is because they then regularly change their earths.

Probably the most unpleasant external parasites are two species of mite, both of which are about a quarter of a millimetre in size (smaller than a full stop on this page). The first is called *Otodectes cynotis*, and it causes otodectic mange (ear canker) in domestic animals. It is found in the ear canal, where several hundred mites, and the resulting accumulation of dirt and wax in the ear, can cause excessive discomfort to the fox. Infected animals will sometimes be seen shaking their heads or scratching vigorously at the base of the ears. Even nastier is sarcoptic mange, caused by *Sarcoptes scabiei*, the same mite that causes scabies in people. It burrows into the fox's skin, where it rapidly multiplies, and by the end of four months the fox will have lost up to a third of its body weight and much of its fur. The skin will be covered with a thick crust of dried body fluids, often over a centimetre thick. These fluids have oozed through the damaged skin, and are full of mites. The animal can by then be infested with several million mites, and be in extreme distress, often gnawing at its infected limbs or tail. In winter it may even enter houses through cat flaps in an attempt to stay warm, having lost a lot of its fur. The fox soon dies, but its body is highly infective in the later stages of mange. When the fox squeezes into an earth or under fences, it deposits bits of crusty skin and mites, and thereby passes the infection to the next fox that passes that way, or even to a pet dog. In areas where mange is prevalent, the fox population can be seriously depleted or even wiped out. When mange first appeared in the foxes living in South Harrow in the 1970s, virtually all the foxes were eliminated in a period of six months, and for some time thereafter foxes were rarely seen in the area.

Not all disease transfer is from foxes to domestic pets; it is quite likely that foxes will become infected by a number of common dog and even cat diseases, for example distemper and parvovirus. They can also become infected with the bacterium (called *Leptospira icterohaemorrhagiae*) that causes Weil's disease; this they catch from eating infected rats or transfer it to each other in their urine. This organism causes serious damage to the fox's kidneys, and in old animals the kidneys may be reduced to nearly half their normal size, very pale, and rather pitted on the surface. The functioning of the kidney is seriously impaired in such cases, and leptospirosis is undoubtedly the final cause of death in many older foxes. One or two other bacterial infections are common causes of death in urban foxes. For instance animals that eat sharp pieces of plastic (see p. 64) may perforate their intestines, and then a bacterial infection of the abdominal cavity will ensue. Similar infections of the chest cavity are quite common in young cubs and adult foxes during the winter months. These infections are usually caused by a bacterium that is quite common in the soil, and presumably the foxes inhale it whilst burrowing or lying up underground. It produces exudative pleurisy; pus and sometimes blood accumulates in the chest cavity of the fox, and it soon dies.

This may sound like a very depressing catalogue, but the important point to remember is that it does not mean that town foxes are any less healthy than rural foxes: country foxes are probably no better off. In fact the majority of town foxes are perfectly healthy; looked at from an alternative viewpoint, 89% of the foxes in Bristol die from something other than disease – and that something is usually man or his cars.

Rabies

One of the biggest fears people have about foxes is that rabies will be reintroduced to this country, and that foxes will become infected and pose a major health hazard. Rabies was endemic in this country in the last century, but then it was largely a disease of domestic animals, and by controlling stray dogs the disease was eventually eliminated in 1903. It was briefly reintroduced to the Plymouth area in 1918 by servicemen returning from the European war zone bringing back infected dogs. The disease spread throughout much of southern England, but again was confined to domestic animals. It was finally eliminated in 1922 after there had been confirmed cases in 312 dogs, 8 cattle, 2 sheep, 3 pigs and 3 horses.

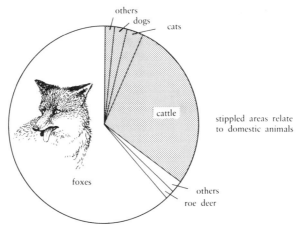

Distribution of rabies cases in France – the majority are in foxes

The current epidemic of rabies in Europe originated in Poland in 1939, and since then has been spreading remorselessly westwards across Europe, recently at a rate of 30 or more kilometres (19 miles) per year. This epidemic differs from the earlier one in that most of the cases are in wild animals, and over 90% of these are foxes. Certainly it is the fox that is responsible for maintaining and spreading the disease. Densities of approximately one fox per square kilometre are sufficient to support the disease, but it is most prevalent in areas where foxes are particularly common. All the control operations in Europe are aimed at eliminating foxes, and in the few places where fox numbers have been drastically reduced the incidence of rabies has fallen dramatically or the disease has been eliminated altogether.

Each year in Britain we hear warnings about the risk of rabies reaching our shores, and people seem to think that the major risk will come when rabies reaches the coastal ports of France. That day cannot be far away, and then the danger will be somewhat enhanced, but we should not think that the risk is not yet present. It certainly is. We are an island, and no animals are allowed in without being put in quarantine. The most likely way that rabies might reach our shores is by someone smuggling in an infected animal. People try to smuggle animals from most parts of the world; rabies is prevalent in much of Europe, Asia, Africa, North and South America, and it is only Britain and a few other countries such as Australia and New Zealand that are currently rabies-free. The lengths to which some people will go to avoid quarantine regulations are incredible. In 1983, for instance, 56 dogs, 36 cats and 17 other mammals were known to be illegally landed in Britain, plus an unknown number of undetected cases. There were 73 prosecutions. One woman spent over a thousand pounds hiring a boat to cross the channel and land her pet dog late one night at an east coast port; she then hired a taxi to drive her home to the Midlands. Fortunately, she was reported to the police by her neighbours. The maximum penalty for avoiding the quarantine regulations under summary proceedings is a fine up to £2,000, or on indictment (where there is evidence of a deliberate intent to evade the provisions) the maximum penalty is an unlimited fine and/or up to one year's imprisonment. Incredible as it may seem, many of the people prosecuted actually seem proud of their fine, since they believe that it shows how devoted they are to their pet. The courts also have the power to order the destruction of the smuggled pet; this they rarely do, but should it become the norm it might be a greater deterrent to offenders than the fine.

Should a rabid pet be successfully smuggled into the country and remain undetected until it becomes infective, its behaviour will change markedly. At first there will be no untoward signs, but later the animal will become irritable or uneasy, and as the disease progresses there may be signs of aggression followed by fits. The animal will try to bite objects or other animals, and will salivate copiously. Finally a progressive paralysis develops, with the animal staggering and finally entering a coma. This pattern is variable, and some animals may only show the terminal stages of the disease. Should rabies be diagnosed in an animal that is not in quarantine, the Ministry of Agriculture, Fisheries and Food then has the unpleasant task of deciding whether there was any chance of the infected animal having spread the disease to other domestic or wild animals, and then setting up a control zone around the source of the incident. Powers to require people to keep all their pet dogs and cats indoors, round up and destroy strays, and enter property to control foxes were all given to the Ministry in the Animal Health Act of 1981. Certainly if the Ministry of Agriculture, Fisheries and Food have to use their powers, the effects on local residents will be severe, and whatever course of action the ministry adopts you can be sure that one lobby or another will be vocal in its criticisms. Muzzling dogs, killing stray dogs and cats and destroying foxes are all unpleasant courses of action, but very necessary to ensure that rabies does not become established in this country. Because of the long period of incubation of the disease, all these restrictions in the control zone would have to continue for six months after the last reported case of rabies to ensure that no infected animals remained.

Should such a course of action ever become necessary, it will be the result of one selfish person smuggling an infected animal into this country, thereby causing massive inconvenience, widespread slaughter and the expenditure of much taxpayers' money. One suggestion frequently made by ill-informed people is that urban foxes should be controlled now in anticipation of rabies reaching this country. Such an idea is totally impractical, and ignores the obvious and simple solution. If everyone obeys the quarantine laws, Britain will remain rabies-free.

Rabies: the disease and its treatment

Rabies is caused by a virus, and most, if not all, species of mammal are susceptible to the disease. Most cases of rabies are the result of a bite wound, when the virus is introduced from the saliva of the infected animal. The deeper the bite wound, the closer it is to the head, and the more heavily muscled the site of the bite wound, the greater is the chance of the victim contracting the disease and the more rapid will be the development of symptoms.

The virus particles travel up the nerves of the victim to the brain, where they multiply, and eventually pass down the nerves to all the organs of the body; by this means some virus particles will travel to the salivary glands. Only then can the virus be passed on, and at this stage the person or animal becomes infective. Virus particles appear in the saliva a day or two before the symptoms of the disease are apparent. The early stages of the disease, before the infective stage, may last only three weeks or, in exceptional circumstances, over a year.

However, once the infective stage is reached, the victim starts to show symptoms of the disease, and death is then inevitable, usually in a few days. If vaccination is arranged soon after being bitten by an infective animal, rabies will be prevented. Obviously the longer the delay before vaccination the greater the risk of the disease developing to its full and fatal extent.

To die from rabies must be horrendous. The final stages of the disease are horrible to watch; patients often have to be restrained, they undergo violent fits and salivate copiously. Muscular spasms prevent them drinking — hence the alternative name hydrophobia. For the victims, the distress cannot be described, since their mental faculties are in no way impaired and they are fully aware of what is happening to them. It is hardly surprising that rabies has been feared by mankind for at least 4,000 years – our earliest records of rabies come from the Babylonian law-makers who, in 2300 BC, imposed heavy penalties on the owners of rabid dogs who did not confine their pets. Throughout the subsequent history of man there are frequent references to rabies, and it was a much feared disease until Louis Pasteur first tried his vaccine in 1885. His vaccine was crude, but in the next fifteen months he treated 2,500 patients; his successes outnumbered his failures. For the first time there was a potential treatment.

Today, modern vaccines are very effective, but expensive to produce. During the present rabies epidemic in western Europe, there have been only a handful of human deaths. Rabies no longer poses a risk to human life, but losses of wild and domestic animals can be considerable. To European man rabies is primarily a financial problem. Compensation for lost livestock, coupled with the costs of control operations, monitoring schemes and vaccination programmes are considerable. In poorer countries, however, these costs cannot be borne, and in India, for instance, at least 15,000 people die each year from rabies (the actual number is probably much higher, since many deaths are not reported). In many countries rabies is still a disease to be feared.

Pesticides and pollutants

We do not know what quantity of pesticides and other pollutants urban foxes are liable to take in with their food, but it is probably quite high. Predators like the fox are most likely to catch weak or dying animals, such as hedgehogs suffering the after effects of eating poisoned slugs and small birds like blue tits dying or weakened after eating caterpillars or aphids sprayed with insecticides. Foxes are at the top of the food chain, and they will accumulate in their own bodies the pesticides present in their prey. They will also eat the caterpillars, beetles, slugs and earthworms for themselves, and all of these can be carrying some of the insecticides that so many gardeners spray liberally on their garden. It would be a fascinating study to see just how many urban foxes are suffering the effects of these pollutants. Certainly I receive numerous reports each year of foxes seen behaving strangely and many of these are suspected of having received a dose of an insecticide or weed-killer.

Some colleagues and I have studied the level of heavy metal pollutants in the foxes living in Bristol. There are several local sources of these substances; one of the major sources of contamination is the smelter at Avonmouth, which is upwind of the city on its western side. This smelter emits smoke and dust containing cadmium, lead and zinc compounds, and there are high levels of airborne contamination as a result. In addition there was a brass works in the city, and, although now redundant, it is still a major source of copper pollution and a secondary source of zinc. In any city the traffic also generates metallic pollutants; tyres contain small quantities of zinc and cadmium and studies in rural Britain have shown that there are increased levels of both these elements in small mammals living near roadsides. Lead is a major pollutant in the exhaust fumes from petrol engines; one estimate suggested that in the northern hemisphere over 350,000 tonnes of lead tetraethyl is burned annually in petrol and thereby introduced into the atmosphere. From there it can be breathed in directly by the foxes (and everything else), or taken in with contaminated food.

With the foxes in Bristol, we discovered that there were high levels of cadmium in the livers and kidneys of animals found around the smelter, and this was most pronounced in older animals. The further away from the smelter the lower the levels of cadmium. Copper and zinc showed irregular distribution patterns throughout the city, since they were derived from a number of different sources. The lead pollution was interesting; the two main sources were the Avonmouth smelter and the road traffic. Lead accumulated in the bones of foxes living near Avonmouth, close to the city centre, or near to busy roads. Obviously the pattern of metal pollution will differ in foxes from other cities, depending on the local sources of pollutants, but there will be a similar pattern of lead pollution from petrol. In America it has been shown that urban dogs have very high levels of lead pollution, which can reach dangerous levels. The dogs (and sometimes urban foxes) are walking along the pavement with their noses at car exhaust level, so perhaps it is not surprising.

In Bristol we found that although there were high levels of metal pollution in many foxes, most were below the level necessary to cause toxicity, although a few old foxes had accumulated harmful levels of cadmium in their kidneys. Other studies have shown that lead pollutants accumulated by city children affect their IQ and school performance. We do not yet know what effects lead pollutants have on the survival of urban foxes – perhaps the first step should be to devise a vulpine IQ test.

The halt and the lame

For a long time it was assumed that a wild animal had to be 100% fit to survive, and that any injury was likely to drastically reduce the animal's chance of survival. More recently many scientists have found that quite a high proportion of the animals they are studying have survived severe injuries in the wild, entirely without the aid of vets and drugs. Whilst I was studying foxes in London I cleaned up the entire skeletons of 331 foxes to see what sort of injuries they had sustained. This largely involved laying the corpses in the sun for the flies and maggots to do their work; as my colleagues at the time will testify, the smell was unforgettable! You do, however, get nice clean skeletons at the end. I found that of the 331 foxes, 91 (27%) had at least one naturally healed bone fracture, and the incidence of injuries increased with age. About 30% of the animals six to twelve months old had at some time suffered from broken bones and now had healed fractures, whereas this figure rose to 70% in animals over five years old. In other words, only about a quarter of urban foxes escape having broken bones by the time they are five years old. Also, there was a slightly higher incidence of healed breaks in male foxes than females. This is presumably because at certain times of the year male foxes are more active than females (see p.98), and so have a greater risk of injury. Often these healed fractures had resulted in the fusion of several adjacent bones or the development of a large bony callous. For instance, breaks to the long bones of the limbs often would not heal at the broken ends; instead the two parts of the broken bone would be pushed together and join at the side where they overlapped. This resulted in a shortening of that part of the leg by up to a third. Alternatively, the break might heal with a bend of up to 30° in the bone.

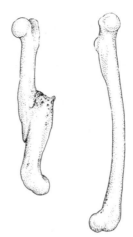

A healed break in a leg bone (femur) of a fox. The broken bone is considerably shorter than the undamaged femur from the same animal.

These injuries sound horrible, yet once healed seem to cause the fox surprisingly little inconvenience, although one consequence of all these injuries was that the foxes were more susceptible to arthritis. Many of the ones I examined had arthritis in the limb, hip and shoulder joints, or around the articulations of the small bones in the feet. The commonest site for arthritis was in the spine; this form of arthritis is called *spondylosis deformans* and is quite frequent in old dogs as well as old people. Of the foxes in London, 35% were affected by spondylosis, again with slightly more male than female foxes suffering, and the males were also more heavily affected than the females. Of the foxes in their third year, 65% had arthritis of the spine, and by six years all the animals were suffering from it. The arthritis was worst in the middle and lower back, and in particularly bad cases the whole spine was fused into a solid mass. The arthritis was worse in animals that had been involved in an accident that had resulted in one or more broken bones.

So how do all these foxes manage to break so many bones? Well, the majority of them are undoubtedly the result of car accidents. Often if an animal had one broken bone, then several others in the same area would also be broken, such as adjacent ribs or several bones in one leg. These sorts of injuries would be the result of a glancing blow from a car, rather than injuries received in fights with other animals. Broken jaw bones and skull fractures were less frequent, and these might sometimes have been the result of fights. In most cases, injuries from cars were to the hind quarters, the sort of injury you would expect if an animal was trying to avoid a motor vehicle. I was once asked if the majority of the injuries were on the left side or the right, since the questioner argued that if the majority were on the left side it would suggest that the foxes checked if a car was coming, started to cross the road, but were unlucky and got caught by a fast moving vehicle on the far side of the road. If the injuries were equally distributed on both sides, he argued, this would indicate that town foxes were jay-walkers. Well, the injuries are equally distributed on both sides, but I do not think his argument about jay-walking holds true. If you watch foxes on the streets at night, they are usually very wary of approaching cars, and when they hear a vehicle coming they will move off the road, often standing just inside a garden gate until the vehicle has passed and they can move back out on to the road. Which makes all these road accidents rather puzzling.

When the injuries first occur, they must render the fox unable to hunt or forage properly, and presumably it will crawl away and lie up under a garden shed or in a nearby earth until the bones start to knit together. Once it is able to feed again, the fox will soon regain its lost weight, and animals with old healed fractures do not weigh less or look in any worse condition than uninjured animals. However, if you watch foxes in a town, do not be surprised to see that quite a few limp or hobble around, and that over 10% in some areas have lost part or all of their tail (the result of a car running over the tail). Some animals even survive the loss of an entire fore or hind leg. These injuries can be quite useful to anyone studying the foxes; they can identify individual foxes by the length of tail remaining and the leg or legs on which the animal limps.

Helping injured foxes

People instantly want to help when they see an injured fox. They imagine that the fox can be caught and kept in a nice warm animal hospital until it is better (it can take several weeks to repair broken bones), and that then the healthy fox can be released back at its home. It sounds good, but there is just one problem: the fox will no longer have a home. Very quickly, once a territory is vacated, another fox will move in to occupy the area – this can happen literally in days. The territory now belongs to the new fox, and the original animal becomes an intruder. If released on its old territory, it will be driven off by the new tenant, and it will be homeless. As I explained on p.77, a homeless fox has much less chance of surviving. So well intended actions may not help an injured fox. Many of the foxes I 'helped' in this way in the past were dead only a few days after they were released.

So what can be done? Unless its injuries are very severe, in which case the animal should be caught and humanely destroyed, it is best to leave the fox alone. Instead, each night put out plenty of food for it, and watch to see how the fox is recovering. Even quite badly injured animals can make an incredibly quick improvement. If this is successful the fox probably has a far better long-term chance of survival than any amount of veterinary care will provide. If you are in any doubt as to what to do, telephone your local branch of the Royal Society for the Prevention of Cruelty to Animals or your local vet for advice (but be warned – my experience of vets is far from good, and most are unwilling to help wild animals since they see no prospect of a fee).

Foxy folklore

Man has hunted foxes for many thousands of years, perhaps nowadays only for fun, but the fox was a major food item for Neolithic man. The remains of red foxes were second only to those of red deer in Stone Age food middens. Written accounts of foxes go back a long way too; Alexander the Great used to hunt them as a relaxation between conquests, and there are several references in the Bible. Salome, in the Song of Solomon, says, 'Bring us the little foxes, for they destroy the grapes.' Perhaps the best known biblical reference is to Samson tying burning brands to the tails of 150 pairs of foxes, and sending them to set fire to the crops of the Philistines. Today we describe foxes with alopecia as 'Samson foxes' because all the hairs are frizzled or singed in appearance, and even the word 'alopecia' is derived from the Greek word for a fox.

From Olaus Magnus (1555): fox feigning death to catch crows, and de-fleaing itself in water while catching crayfish

The fox features prominently in fables (the fox and the crow, the fox and the grapes, etc.) and in mediaeval church carvings. It seemed to be particularly popular with religious sculptors in the late Middle Ages, partly because it was a very well known nuisance with a number of admirable qualities, partly because it had come to symbolize the devil himself and many of his characteristics in an age which was particularly concerned with spiritual values, and partly because the fox was a villainous hero with an international reputation. Many of these early church carvings depict foxes stealing ducks and geese, and invariably show the fox running off with the goose carried across its back. Delightful as this image may be, it is religious licence; foxes do not carry large prey items this way, but rather drag them along the ground.

Quite a few of these mediaeval carvings depict scenes that do have an element of truth about them. The fable of the fox and the grapes tells how the fox was unable to reach a bunch of grapes and wandered off saying that they weren't ripe, anyhow. Many a city dweller who grows his own vines will tell you that foxes love grapes, even when they are not quite ripe, and in some areas their depredations on vines are a major nuisance.

Many of the stories exaggerate the cunning and craftiness of the fox, and should be taken with a very large pinch of salt. It never ceases to amaze me how many of the old country myths about foxes will be repeated by people living right in the middle of a city, usually with the assertion that they have 'seen it themselves'. The commonest is the old chestnut about the fox and the fleas. There are several versions of this; basically the story goes that the fox takes some wool or fur in its mouth, and slowly backs into a pond, so that all the fleas will migrate up to its nose, and eventually on to the piece of wool. The fox finally submerges, releases the wool, and the fleas float away. It would be wonderful if it worked; however, fleas can survive quite long periods of immersion, and since the fur of a fox is very thick it is improbable that the fleas could move up to the nose quickly enough. Anyway, foxes rarely have enough fleas for them to be a problem (see p. 100). Yet I still receive regular reports of foxes reputedly using a garden pond as a de-fleaing tank.

One other tale worth mentioning is how foxes are supposed to catch hedgehogs. The story goes that the fox urinates on the hedgehog to get it to unroll. If you have ever smelt fox urine, you can well believe that the hedgehog would want to unroll and protest, if not gasp for air. I doubt, however, that there is any real basis for the story. The foxes I have seen trying to take living hedgehogs have usually attacked them by repeated bites to the back of the rolled-up animal. Such attacks were unsuccessful, and it is more common to see foxes and hedgehogs hunting earthworms side by side on open lawns, totally ignoring each other. I am sure that most of the hedgehogs that foxes eat are either road casualties or sick hedgehogs that do not roll up completely. It is a pity, since I rather like the urine story.

Pet foxes: don't

Young fox cubs look very appealing, and many people are tempted either to rear a fox cub as a pet, or rescue an apparently orphaned cub with the avowed aim of reintroducing it to the wild when adult. This urge to rear fox cubs is fired by the popular press; each spring they publish pictures of cubs being carried around in shopping bags by beautiful ladies, playing with pet dogs and cats, or even in ludicrous poses curled up with pet rabbits or with chickens sitting on their heads. That's the press for you, but for many people the idea of rearing baby foxes is very attractive.

However tempted you may feel, leave well alone. Each April and May many so-called orphaned fox cubs are reported to animal welfare societies and advice on rearing them sought. Yet many of these cubs are not actually orphaned at all, and should never have been touched. Sometimes a fox cub is left behind when the vixen is moving her cubs from one site to another; if the lost cub is left alone the vixen will often transfer it the following night to the new earth. Whole litters of fox cubs are often assumed to be orphaned simply because the vixen is not with them. Again these cubs are usually quite alright and should be left strictly alone. The normal pattern is for the vixen to stay with her cubs continuously while they are very young. Thereafter the vixen will spend less and less time with her cubs; she will lie up nearby, and return periodically to play with the cubs or to feed them.

Even in situations where the vixen really has been killed, it is often better to leave the cubs where they are. Cubs over six weeks old are able to survive entirely on solid foods, and I know of several instances where the mother was killed and the cubs reared by other members of the family group. Even if other foxes are not able to supply any or enough food for the cubs, it is easiest to leave food outside the earth each day and help to rear the cubs in their own home rather than yours. If they manage to survive until July with a little help, they then should learn to forage for themselves and probably have a good chance of survival, certainly better than if they were reared artificially and then just let go, unprepared, into a hostile world.

Any fox cub that is reared in captivity will quickly become imprinted on its human captors: that is, it will identify them as its 'parents'. When young, the fox will be very playful and give hours of amusement, but as it grows it will become more and more destructive. By late summer the cub will be full-grown, and it will be beyond the resources of most people to keep it. Also, as the fox gets older, it will start to produce its characteristic, powerful smell. This pervades everything, even when the animal is caged out of doors. Each year many people rear cubs to this stage, and then try to get a wildlife park or a zoo to take the fox off their hands. However, such organizations are offered so many foxes each year that they are most unlikely to want any more. Rehabilitating a tame fox to the wild is a difficult and time-consuming task; it can be done, but the animal will never completely lose its familiarity with man. I know of many instances where hand-reared animals have entered farms or gardens during the day, killing pet animals or fowl; their chances of long-term survival are very slim.

So be warned; do not try to rear a fox cub. If you think you have found either a single orphaned cub or an entire litter of orphaned cubs, leave them alone and seek professional advice, preferably from the Royal Society for the Prevention of Cruelty to Animals. If, despite all these warnings, you do try to rear a fox cub, *never* put a collar on it. Each year many cubs escape wearing small cat collars; as the cub grows the collar cuts deeply into its neck, eventually causing a very unpleasant death.

Watching town foxes

In the countryside foxes are very wary of humans and many country dwellers never see a fox other than one being pursued by a pack of hounds. Even if you are lucky enough to locate an earth with a litter of fox cubs in the country, watching them will require a great deal of skill and field craft. The slightest disturbance or hint of danger and the vixen will move her cubs. In a town, watching foxes is a lot easier, and there are several ways to do it.

Probably the simplest way is to locate a litter of cubs; methods for doing this are described on p.121. Young cubs first appear above ground in late April, and often stay in the earth where they were born until early June. After this they are moved away and start to lie up above ground, quite often scattered rather than in a group. So watching them is most profitable in May, with dusk and dawn being particularly rewarding times. Try to select a litter of cubs in a garden, since they will be more tolerant of human activity. If you find a co-operative householder near the cubs, try to obtain permission to watch from an upstairs window overlooking the cubs; such a vantage point is also ideal for photography. Alternatively, a garden shed or even a small tent erected in the garden near the earth will serve as a suitable hide. If you use a tent, leave it for a few days for the foxes to get used to it. With both these sorts of hide you will require a certain degree of field craft; enter your hide before the foxes emerge, and stay there until after the foxes have left, since if they suspect your presence they will be wary. Also you will have to remain very quiet, since foxes have acute hearing. If you need to make a movement, such as raising a camera, do it extremely slowly; foxes are more likely to see sudden movements but not to notice very slow cautious ones.

When the cubs finally desert their earth, they may move to a bramble patch or similar piece of dense cover, where they will remain for the rest of the summer. Although these sites are harder to locate, they are particularly good places to watch, since here the cubs are growing rapidly and developing many of their adult hunting and fighting skills. If you are able to find a building overlooking one of these sites, it will be possible to watch the changing behaviour of the cubs over the space of about three months. By late September they will be difficult to distinguish from their parents; at that stage the cubs will be nearing the time for dispersal, and conflicts within the family group make fascinating watching.

Also try putting out food for the foxes in your garden; after a while if

you keep up a regular supply you should find that they are frequent visitors. They will soon become used to you, and fox watching is far from strenuous when you can sit in your house with a nice bottle of Bordeaux wine and a piece of Shropshire Blue cheese (my personal recommendations), watching foxes a few feet away on the patio. If you do not want to sit and wait for them, tie the food to a fishing line attached to a small bell in the house. The sort used by fishermen at night are ideal – you will soon know when you have a catch. Should you want to illuminate the garden for a better view of the foxes, use a 60 watt light bulb on a flex about 15 metres (50 feet) long, with a bayonet plug on the end. This can easily be inserted into a house light socket and the wire run down the garden and suspended from a tree or washing line. I use such a light a lot and find that the foxes take very little notice of it, even when it is first switched on.

More of a challenge is to find a good foraging site where you can observe them. Spend some time late at night quietly walking the streets in your area until you find a field where the foxes hunt earthworms on wet nights, or a regular crossing point where they will stop and play or greet each other. To watch foxes worming, select a warm wet night, and either use a car as a hide, or position yourself on the far side of the field so that you can see the foxes silhouetted against the street lights along the edge of the field. Low power binoculars with good light gathering capabilities will enable you to watch them clearly. A car is also a useful hide for watching foxes playing on the streets at night. Try to find a profitable spot, and then put some bait on the edge of the road or on the pavement in an attempt to keep the foxes in view for a while. For this I use aniseed balls; foxes love them.

If you really want the foxes to use your garden regularly, try to provide some cover so that they use it as a daytime refuge. A nice patch of bramble at the bottom of the garden is ideal, or you can even build them an artificial earth. This is quite easy; dig out an earth chamber about a metre (3 feet) in diameter and 35 centimetres (14 inches) high, preferably in a bank or piece of sloping ground. A board or piece of metal will do for the roof, with about 50 to 70 centimetres (20 to 28 inches) of soil on top of this. Build two entrance holes, connected to the surface with old drain pipes about 22 centimeters (9 inches) in diameter and at least a metre and a half long (5 feet). Keep it simple; if the foxes like it they will alter the earth to suit their requirements, and then you may well be lucky enough to have cubs born in your garden each year.

Studying town foxes

In this book I have tried to give a brief overview of our knowledge about urban foxes. This is based largely on studies in just a few urban areas, and in several places I have indicated where there are variations in the behaviour of foxes living in different cities. We still do not really know why these differences exist, and it is only by gathering information from many more towns that we can fully understand the behaviour of urban foxes.

Although much of the information in this book has been gleaned from many years of hard field work using expensive equipment, there are still many things that a keen amateur can do to add to our fund of knowledge.

Fresh (dark)

Dry (whitish)

Fox droppings – fresh ones are brown but older ones become much paler and more brittle.

For instance, you could scour the areas where foxes are common and collect their faeces (see illustration). Store the faeces dry, individually labelled with the date and locality. When you have a few, it is easy to analyse the contents of the droppings. All you really need is a simple microscope, and many schools or local museums will help you here. Soak the faeces overnight in some water to soften them, and in the morning stir them vigorously until they are completely broken up. Let the contents settle and then use a small pipette to spread a few drops of the sediment on a microscope slide. If the fox has been eating earthworms you will see lots of yellow or orange-coloured 'chaetae' (the little bristles that are found in the earthworm's skin). Under the low power of a microscope they look like little daggers. Wash the rest of the faecal remains through a fine sieve or piece of old

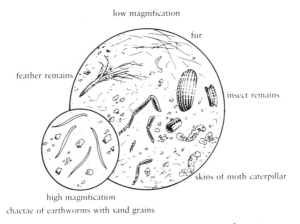

low magnification

fur

feather remains

insect remains

high magnification

skins of moth caterpillar

chaetae of earthworms with sand grains

Food remains from fox droppings as seen under microscope

stocking until they are clean, put them in a white enamel dish, and cover with water. This makes it easier to recognize the bits. The remains of beetles and bones are easy to identify; hairs and feathers are a little more tricky, and you need a key. Get the local library to order you a copy of the paper by Day given in the bibliography. To make the most of your efforts, try to quantify what you find; score everything you see on a scale of one to five, depending on how much there is, and then it will give you some idea of the importance of the different food items.

You could complement this food study with a door-to-door survey to see what damage the foxes are doing in your area. Design a questionnaire (keep it fairly simple so as not to dissuade people from helping), and go round to the houses to collect your information. To be of real value, you should obtain a return from every house, not just those that have something definite to say. That way you can find out how many pet cats, rabbits, etc., the foxes are killing, or what proportion of the households have their dustbins rifled by the foxes. Undoubtedly you will find the results surprising. You could also try to find out how many people are feeding the foxes in your area, how much food and what sort they are putting out. If your results are anything like mine, you will probably start to wonder why your local foxes are not grossly overweight. And it's all high cholesterol food as well.

To find out how many foxes you actually have in your area, you will need to do a fox cub survey (see p.90). This involves locating all the litters of fox cubs born in a particular area. It should be done in late April and early May, and will require a lot of keen helpers. First of all you should deliver a circular to all the houses requesting sightings of fox cubs to be reported. While delivering the circulars make a list of all the pieces of derelict land, factory sites and overgrown gardens in the area; these should be systematically searched to see if any of them is sheltering a family of foxes. The sort of situations in which the foxes are likely to rear cubs are described on p.45. Time is critical, so complete your survey quickly. Foxes are newsworthy, so try to interest the local paper in publicizing your survey. At the end you will know the locations of all the litters of cubs and how many there are; this will tell you how many families of foxes are present. With enough interested helpers, you may even be able to extend your survey to cover quite a large area.

Once you have located your litters of cubs, you will then have an opportunity to select those that are easy to watch (see p.117 for some tips) and study them in detail. By careful observation you can learn to recognize individual foxes, and then see how many cubs and adults are present in the family group. Observations over two or three consecutive years will show you what changes occur, and give you some idea of the average litter size and family group structure in your area.

The adult foxes will also bring food back to the cubs; small food items will be consumed entirely, whilst feathers, fur and bones will be left from larger prey items. By careful watching, you can identify the number and types of food items brought to the cubs by the adults. Also, you can carefully explore the area around the earth every few days and catalogue the food debris that remains. Then see how these results differ from your visual observations. But be careful; if you disturb the earth itself the vixen may move the cubs elsewhere, although urban foxes are generally more tolerant than rural foxes of human activity around their earth.

It will not take you long to collect some valuable data. This is only the first step, however; it is most important that you publish your results somewhere, so that others can benefit from your efforts. There is a list of societies on p.123, and by contacting any of these you will get invaluable advice first on how to organize your study and then on how to write up and publish your findings. Good luck!

Useful societies

If you are interested in learning more about mammals in general or foxes in particular, then you really should join the Mammal Society; membership details can be obtained from The Secretary, The Mammal Society, Burlington House, Piccadilly, London W1V 0LQ. The society produces a variety of publications, organizes national and regional meetings, and has a group specializing in the study of carnivores. It also has a youth group for younger members.

In recent years the study of urban wildlife has become very popular, and there are now urban wildlife groups active in about twenty towns and cities throughout Britain. These groups organize surveys and projects, and create or manage wildlife habitats in our urban areas. In London there is the London Wildlife Trust, 80 York Way, London N1 9AG, in Birmingham the Urban Wildlife Group, 11 Albert Street, Birmingham B4 7UA and in Bristol the Avon Wildlife Trust, The Old Police Station, 2 Jacobs Wells Road, Bristol BS8 1DR. Details of these and all the other urban wildlife groups can be obtained from the Royal Society for Nature Conservation, The Green, Nettleham, Lincoln NS2 2NR. This society will also supply information on your County Naturalists' Trust (you should undoubtedly be a member of your County Naturalist Trust if you are not already), and the RSNC also sponsors the WATCH club for under-18s. This club organizes a variety of projects, many of which are applicable to urban areas.

The Nature Conservancy Council, Northminster House, Peterborough PE1 1UA, produces a number of useful booklets on urban wildlife, urban habitat surveys and urban nature conservation; they will send you a complete list of their publications on request.

Bibliography

Below is a list of books which will give you further information about foxes, mammals in general, urban wildlife and urban ecology; most will be obtainable through your local library.

The Red Fox by H.G. Lloyd (Batsford, London, 1980). A very detailed and comprehensive account of the biology of foxes.

Fox Family by M. Taketazu (Weatherhill, New York, 1979). A book of outstanding fox photographs taken in Japan. Highly recommended.

The Handbook of British Mammals, second edition, edited by G.B. Corbet and H.N. Southern (Blackwell Scientific Publications, Oxford, 1977). A definitive account of all British mammals, although now a little dated; new edition will be compiled shortly. The first edition, edited by H.N. Southern and published in 1964, includes some very useful chapters on techniques for studying mammals, but these were omitted from the second edition.

Rabies and Wildlife by D.W. Macdonald (Oxford University Press, Oxford, 1980). An account of rabies in wildlife and the possible methods of control.

Wild Dogs of the World by L.E. Bueler (Constable, London, 1974). A useful synopsis of the biology of all the species of wild dog in the world.

Discovering Doorstep Wildlife by J. Feltwell (Hamlyn, Twickenham, 1985). A recent guide to the diversity of wildlife found in cities; there are many other books covering the same subject.

How to Make a Wildlife Garden by C. Baines (Elm Tree Books, London, 1985). Gives helpful hints on how to improve the diversity of wildlife in your garden.

Wildlife in towns: a teachers' guide by T. Sames (Nature Conservancy Council, Peterborough, 1982). An invaluable aid to teachers who wish to enhance their pupils' awareness of the urban wildlife in their area.

'Identification of hair and feather remains in the gut and faeces of stoats and weasels' by M.G. Day (published in the *Journal of Zoology*, London, vol. 148, pp. 201–217, in 1966). An indispensable guide for anyone trying to identify food remains in fox faeces – see p. 121.

Index

If you have enjoyed this book, you might be interested to know about other titles in our **British Natural History** series:

BADGERS
by Michael Clark
with illustrations by the author

BATS
by Phil Richardson
with illustrations by Guy Troughton

DEER
by Norma Chapman
with illustrations by Diana E. Brown

EAGLES
by John A. Love
with illustrations by the author

FROGS AND TOADS
by Trevor Beebee
with illustrations by Guy Troughton

GARDEN CREEPY-CRAWLIES
by Michael Chinery
with illustrations by Guy Troughton

HEDGEHOGS
by Pat Morris
with illustrations by Guy Troughton

OWLS
by Chris Mead
with illustrations by Guy Troughton

RABBITS AND HARES
by Anne McBride
with illustrations by Guy Troughton

ROBINS
by Chris Mead
with illustrations by Kevin Baker

SEALS
by Sheila Anderson
with illustrations by Guy Troughton

SNAKES AND LIZARDS
by Tom Langton
with illustrations by Denys Ovenden

SQUIRRELS
by Jessica Holm
with illustrations by Guy Troughton

STOATS AND WEASELS
by Paddy Sleeman
with illustrations by Guy Troughton

WHALES
by Peter Evans
with illustrations by Euan Dunn

WILDCATS
by Mike Tomkies
with illustrations by Denys Ovenden

Each title is priced at £6.95 at time of going to press. If you wish to order a copy or copies, please send a cheque, adding £1 for post and packing, to Whittet Books Ltd, 18 Anley Road, London W14 OBY. For a free catalogue, send s.a.e. to this address.